The Crystal Files: Mission Aquamarine

Timothy Wolfe

StoryLight Press

Illustrations by Lucy Perterson

thecrystalfiles.com

Publisher's Cataloging-in-Publication Data

Names: Wolfe, Timothy, author.
Title: Mission aquamarine / Timothy Wolfe.
Series: The Crystal Files
Description: Glen Allen, VA: StoryLight Press, 2025. | Summary: Kyle always knew his past held mysteries, but when he gets a necklace for his birthday, he realizes that his past might hold an even more sinister secret.
Identifiers: LCCN: 2025912559 | ISBN: 978-1-967640-00-3 (hardcover) | 978-1-967640-06-5 (paperback) | 978-1-967640-05-8 (ebook)
Subjects: LCSH Friendship--Fiction. | Family--Fiction. | Adoption--Fiction. | Adventure fiction. | Mystery fiction. | Christian fiction. | BISAC JUVENILE FICTION / Action & Adventure / General | JUVENILE FICTION / Family / Adoption | JUVENILE FICTION / Religious / Christian / General | JUVENILE FICTION / Social Themes / General
Classification: LCC PZ7.1 .W65 Mi 2025 | DDC [Fic]--dc23

Contents

The Dolphin Diamond

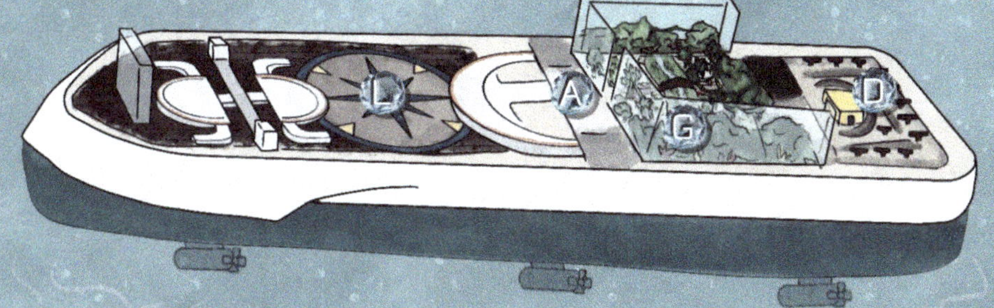

Sapphire Deck

Amber Deck

Emerald Deck

Main Deck

A Aqariums

B Bravo's Bistro

C Cabin

D Dolphin Diner

G Gardens

J Jewlery Shop

L Lobby

P Pool

T Treehouse

"Agent Young to the office." The voice crackled over the PA system, and Young quickly saved a file before closing the laptop and getting up. A summon to the office was never to be ignored. That had been one of the first things the Rose had drilled into them. Ignoring the glances from the other agents, Young walked briskly across the carpeted room and into the cavernous marble hallway.

Reaching the large double oak doors of the office, the agent wasted no time in sliding a badge over the sensor. The light clicked green, and the doors slowly swung outward, revealing the large, mahogany-paneled room, which could have been a small apartment if not for the huge, crystal chandelier and the hundreds of antique bookshelves lining the walls. The director sat behind a state-of-the-art computer setup, her dark gaze fixed on Young.

"Agent Young, would you care to explain this to me?" she asked lightly, although a threat lurked beneath her words. Turning to a monitor built into her desk, she began to read. "'Monday, around midnight, a ten-year-old boy was found on the beach by a senior officer of the Maine State Police. According to the report filed after the incident, the boy and his parents had been out sailing and had ignored warnings of an approaching storm surge. During the storm, the boat capsized and both parents were killed. However, the boy miraculously survived.'"

Young put on a show of calm, but inside, the agent's heart was racing. "You're calling me out on a gig I did two years ago?"

"Hold on; there's more." The director raised an eyebrow, though her expression was far from amused. "'Having no other close living relatives, the boy has since been taken in by Fiona Sanders, a longtime friend of his mother.' The Fiona Sanders who, may I remind you" —the director pressed a button, and the screen retracted into her desk, leaving Young no choice but to stare directly at the director— "should have been *dead*." The word hung in the air like a bomb about to explode.

No excuse Young could think up would satisfy the director. A simple "she got away" wouldn't cut it. Young braced for the dreaded words: *"We're letting you go."* Two years of preparation and hard work would slip through the agent's fingers like sand.

"Young, we cannot accept failure, but *hiding* failure is out of the question. However, the counsel has decided to give you grace, on one condition."

Just as quickly as the agent's hope had risen, it fell.

"You must finish this mission. Fiona Sanders, whom we will refer to as the 'Weed' from now on, will be leaving on a cruise with the boy, Kyle Sanders. We have already placed you in a position in which you will have access to both parties. You leave in five days. All of the information is located in this file." The director slid a micro SD card over the desk. "You are dismissed."

Young took the card and was almost to the door when the director's voice came from behind.

"And Young, don't fail again."

Young watched the reflection in the polished door give a knowing smirk. "Don't worry. This time, she won't be able to run."

1

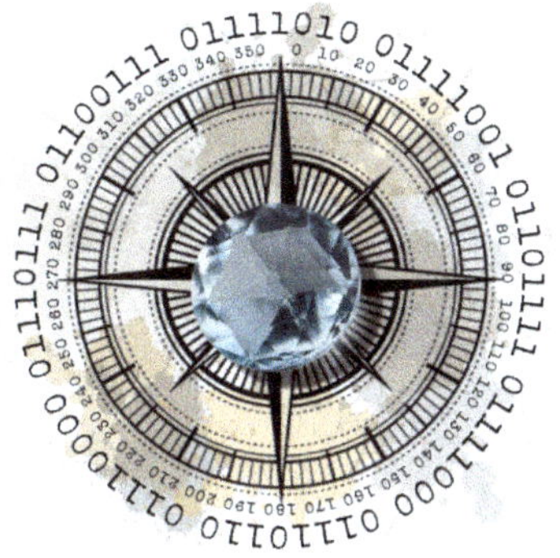

KYLE LOOKED OUT OVER the water, letting the small waves lap at his bare feet. Tomorrow he would be out there on the ocean for the first time in years. A cold chill went up his spine, despite the humid Florida heat.

"Kyle!" his adoptive mom called from the house.

He knew he should call back to let her know where he was, but right now he just wanted to be alone.

Footsteps approached, and he sighed as Mrs. Sanders sat down beside him, making the old boards creak.

"How are you feeling?" she asked gently.

Kyle kicked at the water. "Fine, I guess." He couldn't let her know that he was scared. She must have spent a fortune on the cruise. He should've been thrilled, but really, he dreaded it.

"Come on, Kyle. You're not acting very excited."

He didn't respond. Instead, he just picked at the splintering wood of the pier.

"It's not going to be like last time. It's like a floating city. You won't even know you're on a boat."

"What if I do, though?" Kyle asked, turning to look at her. The moonlight made her dirty-blonde hair look almost white.

"Trust me, you won't." Without warning, she put an arm around him, and he tensed. "It's going to be great, Kyle. You just have to trust me."

Kyle looked down. It wasn't fair that she hadn't asked him if he wanted to go. She had just announced a week ago that they were going, and that was that. He still couldn't imagine why she had signed him up in the first place. They'd both seen what had happened the last time he had gotten on a boat.

Something his psychologist had said after the accident flashed through his mind. *If you want to get over your fear, you have to face it.* Maybe Mrs. Sanders was right. Maybe it would be good to be back on the ocean. *After all, it's just for eight days.*

"Come on," Mrs. Sanders said, standing up and yawning. "It's getting late. I'm going to turn in." She gave him a pointed look he knew meant, "and so should you."

"I'll come in a little bit." Sometimes he hated himself for wanting to be alone. Though it wasn't like anyone else understood him.

"All right. I'll come and get you in ten minutes if you're not back by then." She headed back to the house, her footsteps fading into the sea wind.

Turning back to the water, Kyle noticed something he hadn't before. Far off on the ocean was a mass of dark gray clouds, pinpricks of light flashing inside of it. *A storm.* The air suddenly felt cold. He could almost imagine one of the whitecaps beyond the inlet was a sailboat.

Getting up, he started toward the house, trying to ignore the distant roll of thunder. However, he couldn't block out the cold ache where his parents had been. Maybe it was time to face his fear and his past. Maybe then it wouldn't haunt him.

T HE NEXT MORNING FLEW by in a flurry of excitement and chaos. After a quick breakfast, they packed everything into the car, and peeled out of the driveway. Two hours and a bathroom break later, they pulled into the crowded parking garage. Another half hour passed before they finally found a spot. By the time they made it to the terminal, he was already sweating from the humidity. Stepping inside, a blast of frigid air washed over him and goosebumps immediately ran up his arms.

Mrs. Sanders let out a contented sigh, grinning at Kyle. "Ahhh... air conditioning. Come on, the line's this way."

Kyle lugged his suitcase behind him, following her to the long line of people.

Mrs. Sanders sighed, setting her suitcase down. "This might take a while. You can wait over there for me." She nodded toward a row of black cushioned chairs.

Nodding, he sat down in the nearest unoccupied seat, keeping a few chairs between him and a girl about his own age. Swinging his backpack down to the floor, he turned in his seat, trying to get at least a glimpse of the ship through the windows behind him. All that greeted him, though, was a concrete dock filled with machinery, crates, and workers disappearing around the building.

"Are you excited?"

Kyle jumped, turning to face the girl beside him, who was now looking at him expectantly.

"Uh, yeah," he replied, regaining himself. Then he winced. That was all he could come up with? *Yeah*?

The girl looked at Kyle for a few more seconds, then glanced away.

"Which line are you going on?" Kyle asked, trying to start the conversation up again. "I mean ship. *Cruise* ship." Kyle stared at the floor. *Smooth.* Why had he said *line*?

"Oh." The girl replied, eyes lighting up. "It's the *Dolphin Diamond*."

"Ocean, it's our turn," a bearded man called to her from in front of one of the reception desks.

"Hey, wait, that's—" Kyle stopped as the girl, Ocean, stood up, and he noticed for the first time that she only had one leg. The other one was replaced with a metal rod connecting her shoe to her knee. Glancing back at him, the girl saw his expression, and a flicker of pain crossed her face. Kyle turned away, his face heating up as he focused his attention on the reception desk.

"And here's your wrist bands." The receptionist said dryly, handing two blue bracelets with shiny chips to Mrs. Sanders. "These will let you into your room and allow you to purchase items during the cruise. You can add money at the check-in desk. *Next!*"

Mrs. Sanders walked over to where Kyle was sitting.

"Looks like *someone* hasn't had a good day." She smiled.

"Yeah," Kyle agreed, wondering for a brief moment whether she meant the receptionist or him. He glanced at Ocean, who was now going through security. He quickly turned away.

"Come on, Kyle," Mrs. Sanders called.

Kyle grabbed his suitcase and backpack and he followed her toward the line of people leading to the metal detectors. He tried to ignore Ocean as she moved through the line, and he was relieved when she disappeared past the scanners.

"This is much faster than an airport security line," Mrs. Sanders commented, and Kyle had to agree, though he had only been on a plane once.

He shut his eyes tight to try to block out the memory, but it didn't help. He could still remember that day so vividly.

Ten-year-old Kyle stepped through the metal detector, not looking up. He felt completely empty inside, like something had been ripped out of him and the wound had sealed shut. He barely heard Mr. Jenkins trying to comfort him.

"Kyle, I know you feel lonely and scared, but I'm sure you'll like Mrs. Sanders. She's really nice. She's really looking forward to meeting you."

Kyle swallowed hard and bit his lip to stop himself from crying again. Mr. Jenkins didn't know how it felt. How could he? No one could imagine what losing someone felt like until they actually lost someone.

"Kyle, can you come to the bench and take off your jacket? You're holding up the line."

Kyle took a deep breath to compose himself, and walked over to a red and green bench leaning against the wall. He unzipped his jacket slowly, then placed it on the bench. He looked up at Mr. Jenkins, not really knowing why. Maybe to see his kind, reassuring face. Mr. Jenkins looked down at Kyle sympathetically.

"I know this is really hard for you. You're very brave, Kyle. Not very many other kids I've taken in are as brave as you."

"Flight 472 to Tampa, Florida, will now begin boarding," a woman's voice blared out of the ceiling.

"That's us," Mr. Jenkins said, taking his duffle bag and Kyle's carry-on suitcase and backpack off the conveyor belt. After a guard had inspected his jacket, Kyle slipped it back on and zipped it up. Then he stood, and walked toward the gate leading to a new life.

"Kyle," Mrs. Sanders said, shaking Kyle out of his daydream.

He blinked a couple of times, coming back to reality.

"Are you okay?" Her blue eyes stared at him softly, and he glanced away, hearing her sigh from beside him.

"Come on. It's our turn," she said.

The guard was motioning for them to come forward. Kyle placed his carry-on suitcase and backpack on the conveyor belt and walked through the metal detector, followed by Mrs. Sanders. After retrieving their luggage, they started toward a white corridor with windows on the left that looked out at a huge sleek white cruise ship.

"There it is!" announced Kyle, shaking off the feelings from his memory as he gazed at the *Dolphin Diamond*. It was connected to the terminal by a long, slanting, glass walkway with a worn, dark blue carpet.

As he stepped onto the gangway, his stomach did a flip. He tried not to look at the water as he fell in step with Mrs. Sanders.

"You ready for this?" Mrs. Sanders asked, looking down at him, concerned.

Kyle took a deep breath, pushing the dread down in his stomach. *I can't be afraid forever.* Slowly, he nodded, bracing himself as he walked through the large rectangular opening and into the ship.

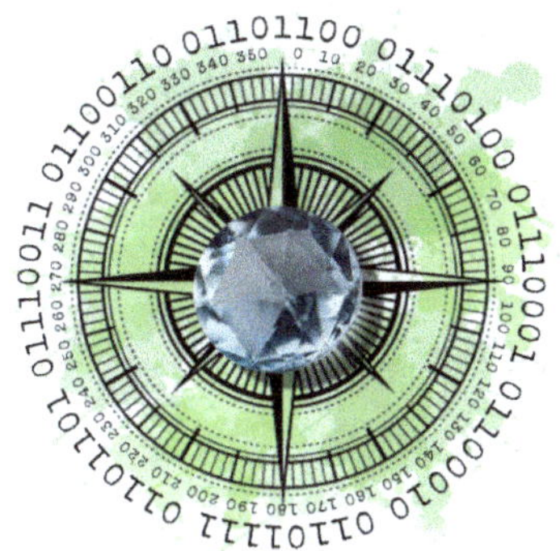

2

KYLE GAZED AROUND HIM in wonder, his mouth hanging open. Yellow light shone from three huge crystal chandeliers in the center of the lobby, glinting off two spiral staircases with mother-of-pearl railings and clear glass steps. On the polished marble floor rested an ornate dolphin fountain, nestled below the chandeliers. A dozen shops and vendors lined the outside of the lobby.

Kyle tried to take in everything around him at once. Mrs. Sanders seemed to be just as awed as she slowly spun around.

"Well," she said, breaking the silence, or semi-silence because of the buzzing, chatting crowds, "I'm going to go check us in; why don't you wait by the fountain over there?"

"Uh... okay." Kyle glanced at a small group of tourists already gathered around the fountain.

"Good. This shouldn't take long." With that, she headed off in the direction of the booths.

Kyle approached the fountain, gazing at the brass statue of three dolphins leaping out of sea spray, water streaming from their mouths and casting ripples over the aquamarine stones at the bottom.

"Look at this, Cora," a woman exclaimed. "There's a *park* on the ship!"

Kyle turned to see the tourist group now gathered around an ornately carved wooden signpost. *A park? On a cruise ship?* Of course, it wasn't like he had ever been on a cruise ship before. For all he knew, all cruise ships had one.

"Come on, Mom! You said we could get something on the ship," a boy from the group complained.

"Alright. Maybe there's a vendor somewhere."

"Or we could just wait until lunch," a man, probably the father, grumbled.

As the group walked away across the lobby, a pang of longing filled Kyle. He could almost imagine himself living in a *real* family. No, not just imagine it. He could *remember* it.

He remembered how his mom had taken him out for ice cream at Black Berry Creamery. How his dad had taken him out on their small yacht, so he could do his schoolwork on the ocean, and would teach him things about wood carving, dolphins, sharks, and how the cliffs were formed by erosion. How his dad would take out his Bible on trips like that, teaching from it, or just reading a verse that seemed to fit into what he was learning. They would listen to the waves crashing on the cliffs, and feel the boat rock back and forth, surrounded by nothing but water.

Kyle's heart sank remembering all of this. Sure, he could still read the Bible, but what was the point? It was like everything else. The ice cream place, wood carving, even school had lost its color when his parents died.

Kyle sat down on the cool marble rim of the fountain and took a deep breath. That was all two years ago. He *had* to stop thinking about it. They were gone. He couldn't keep it from happening, because it already happened, and now Mrs. Sanders was his mom. Kyle grimaced. Those were almost the same words the therapist had used.

He shook his head to stop his mind from wandering there and looked up at the map that the other group had been standing in front of.

"Checking out the ship *already*?" came a voice from behind him, making him jump.

"Oh, hi," Kyle said, turning around to see Mrs. Sanders standing there, smirking. Would he ever get used to her sneaking up on him?

A voice suddenly crackled to life from a speaker above them. "This is your captain speaking. Welcome aboard the *Dolphin Diamond*, a ship full of adventures to come and a vast array of entertainment. We will be leaving in just under thirty minutes. Make sure to check in before departure, or we might just leave you behind. Just kidding, however you will not be able to get into your room so we still highly recommend checking in. *Thank you* for choosing Crystal Compass Cruise Lines! We will not disappoint you."

At this, the voices around them seemed to suddenly rise.

"Wow! Two hundred people sure can make a *lot* of noise," Mrs. Sanders commented, raising her voice to be heard over the chattering.

"Maybe we could go to our rooms and unpack," Kyle suggested, taking a deep breath to block out the increasing buzz around them. "We can be back before the ship leaves."

"I doubt that any of our stuff is going to be there." She looked at him curiously, and he inwardly winced.

"We can still unpack our carry-ons," he said, trying to cover his mistake.

"That's my boy," Mrs. Sanders said, stroking Kyle's hair.

Kyle jerked away. He was *not* her boy. He would never be.

"Sorry," Mrs. Sanders said just loud enough to be heard over the crowd.

A flash of guilt flooded him, even though she *wasn't* his mother. He only had one mother and she was gone.

"Anyway, our room is this way," Mrs. Sanders said, starting toward the crystal stairs.

Kyle silently grabbed his suitcase awkwardly from next to the fountain, then followed Mrs. Sanders across the giant floor, toward the clear, gleaming staircase that curved below another dazzling chandelier. As they stepped onto the reddish-brown wood of the balcony, Kyle ran his hand over the smooth railing looking out over the lobby. Peering down at the earth-patterned marble, he could make out a compass pattern spanning the entire floor in spite of the people scattered over it. Each protruding spike ended in glistening white letters.

"Oh, wow..." Mrs. Sanders breathed. "Isn't it gorgeous up here?"

"Yeah." He definitely had to agree.

"Well, come on. Our room *awaits*!"

Kyle took one last look at the lobby, then followed her into the glass elevator waiting for them, already crowded with people. Through the glass, he caught sight of someone staring at him and he froze, his heart starting to beat faster, though just as quickly, the person was lost in the crowd. He shook his head as his heart rate started to return to normal. The person had probably been staring at the elevator, or maybe someone else on the elevator. Why would anyone be staring at him?

THE SCENT OF FRESH oranges wafted through the air as Mrs. Sanders and Kyle stepped through the dark wooden door of their cabin.

"Look at that *view*!" Mrs. Sanders exclaimed.

Kyle turned to gaze out a square window. The port bustled below them, partially blocked out by the gravel roof of the terminal.

"This will be beautiful once we're on the ocean."

He tried to imagine what it would be like to see nothing but ocean every time he looked out his window. The thought sent a jolt of fear through him. They were about to sail out onto the ocean. Hopefully Mrs. Sanders was right about it not being like last time.

Turning away, Kyle set down his carry-on, raced past the dark maple closet on his right, and flung himself onto the bed. He sank into the soft mattress. Breathing deep, he inhaled the fresh smell of lavender, then rolled over on his back and closed his eyes.

"Kyle! Come look at this." Mrs. Sanders's voice echoed from somewhere in front of him.

Curious, Kyle opened his eyes and propelled himself off the bed, causing something to tumble onto the floor. Landing on the soft carpet, he saw a folded piece of paper and picked it up, reading the title to himself.

"Welcome to the Dolphin Diamond!"

Just out of curiosity, he flipped it over and read the short introduction.

"Hi! I hope your stay on the Dolphin Diamond *has been going well! I'm Emily, your personal assistant, and I'll be taking care of your room while you're gone. If you have any questions, I would be delighted to answer them all! Just press the gray button on the intercom. Thank you for sailing with Crystal Compass Cruise Lines!"*

Placing the note on the bedside table next to the intercom, Kyle turned around and saw light pouring through the now open bathroom door. He padded over to the door and stepped onto a gleaming floor of white and cloudy-blue tiles.

Mrs. Sanders stood in front of a bathtub, looking at something on the counter next to one of the sinks. "Isn't this gorgeous?" she asked, turning to Kyle.

Kyle walked over to Mrs. Sanders, and examined the object on the counter. "Wow," he breathed, gazing at the white rose soap carving, sitting in a clear rose-patterned soap dish. "Do you think we're supposed to use it?"

"Hmm..." Mrs. Sanders picked the soap up and turned it over. On the bottom Kyle saw a yellow piece of paper. Leaning over, he could barely make out the words:

This soap was hand-carved by the Crystal Carving Center.

> *Please feel free to use this gift from us.*
> *~Crystal Compass Cruise Line*
> *"We're delighted to serve you."*

"Well, there's your answer," Mrs. Sanders concluded, placing the soap back on the tray.

Kyle turned toward the tall light-brown closet, standing against the wall. "I wonder what's in there," he mused as he pulled open the door.

"Probably extra blankets, soap, toilet paper..."

As Mrs. Sanders continued, Kyle scanned the shelves.

"...A skeleton, spiders, perhaps a gorilla or two..."

Unable to help himself, Kyle burst out laughing.

Mrs. Sanders grinned. "I thought you weren't listening."

"I—" He suddenly stopped, remembering in a flash laughing with his mother when he had accidentally poured half a jar of peanut butter on his bread. He looked down at the cold tiles.

"Well, let's go unpack," Mrs. Sanders suggested after a minute, the joy in her voice gone as she closed the closet door.

Heat flooded his face as he followed her out of the bathroom and onto the soft maroon carpet of the main bedroom. It wasn't his fault. Why did she have to try to get closer to him? Why couldn't she understand that he didn't want her to be his mom?

"Kyle..." Mrs. Sanders began, and he looked up to see her quickly hide the hurt on her face. "Welcome to your new room."

3

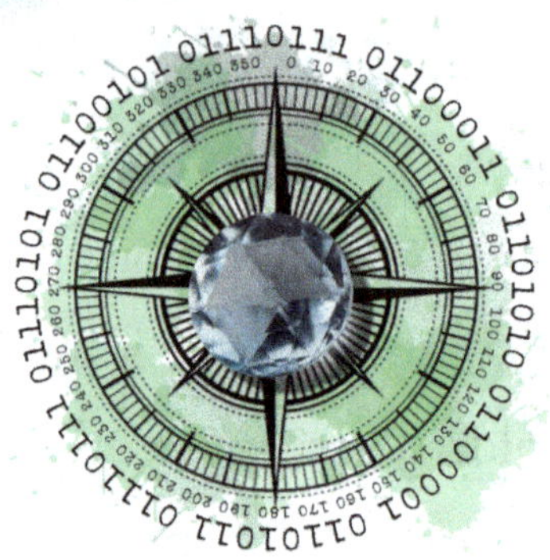

K YLE GRABBED HIS SUITCASE from next to the bathroom door and padded over to where Mrs. Sanders stood in front of her bedside table.

"How about I get the drawer to the left of the bed, and you get the right one," she suggested.

"Okay." Kyle shrugged and unzipped the suitcase, laying it on its back. He was about to start unpacking, then he stopped, reached inside and pulled out a navy blue pajama shirt. He gave it a curious look. How had that gotten in there?

"Uh...Mom?" His stomach turned at the name she had insisted he call her. "Is this supposed to be in here?"

"Yep." She smiled. "I got it for you before the trip. Do you like it?"

"Umm..." He looked the shirt over, not wanting to make her feel bad. "Yeah."

"Turn it inside out."

"Okay…" Kyle frowned, but did as she said. The shirt was now a light gray with a dark-gray embroidered dolphin jumping out of a wave under a crescent moon. He couldn't help but smile.

"You like it?" Crinkles formed around her blue eyes as she smiled back. "There are pants in the suitcase that match it."

Kyle turned back to the suitcase and started searching through it, moving three books, a flashlight, and his toiletry pouch out of the way before pulling out a pair of soft, navy-blue pants. Embroidered on the right knee was another dolphin, this one fat and much lighter gray than the one on the shirt, with shimmering bubbles surrounding it. A dolphin calf.

He looked up at Mrs. Sanders, knowing he should say something. "Thanks," he said, avoiding her gaze.

"Hold on. There's one more thing." She disappeared behind the bed, emerging a few seconds later holding a small box wrapped in gold paper.

Kyle reached out to take it, but he stopped when he saw Mrs. Sanders's expression. A solemn, almost sad look had replaced her usual carefree smile.

"Kyle…" She trailed off, then cleared her throat. "This one's from your mother."

Kyle's heart froze. He looked at her for an explanation, but instead she just held out the box, forcing a smile.

"You'll understand when you open it," she said, handing it to him.

He was almost afraid to touch it. It felt wrong somehow to open something his mother had wrapped for him. Mrs. Sanders said nothing as he tore open the paper, uncovering the box underneath. Embossed on the top was a painted silver silhouette of a dolphin leaping out of the water. Carefully, he lifted it off. Inside, a glittering silver chain and an intricate wooden dolphin rested on top of velvet padding. His breath caught in his throat as he rubbed his finger along the smooth back.

Glancing up, he saw Mrs. Sanders looking away. After a few seconds she turned to him, her eyes glossy.

"This necklace was your mother's. Your father carved it for her as a wedding gift."

He glanced back down at the necklace. *This is my mother's.* He slowly lifted it out and Mrs. Sanders continued.

"This is the only piece of jewelry that didn't go to your trust fund. I thought you would like to have it. It has a part of your father and your mother in it."

Tears welled up in Kyle's eyes and he looked away. Was it wrong that he felt guilty about having it? The prick of homesickness filled him as he held the necklace up to the sunlight and imagined his father's rough hands intricately carving it and his mother wearing it on the deck of the *Emerald Wind* as the sea air whipped around her dress.

"Thanks," Kyle whispered, closing his eyes as tears rolled down his cheeks.

"Attention," boomed a voice from a speaker in the ceiling, making Kyle jump. "This is your captain speaking; we will be leaving in fifteen minutes. Please feel free to walk around the ship. However, I suggest heading for the front of the lobby, where you can watch the departure through our state-of-the-art glass hull. You can also view the departure from the Sapphire Deck. Please note that the swimming pools will be closed until 12:30. If you have any questions, feel free to ask any of our staff about the ship. Let's get this adventure started!"

Mrs. Sanders looked like she was about to say more, but then she shook her head. "Well, come on. Unpacking can wait. Right now, let's head over to the main lobby. You don't want to miss this." She tried to sound excited, but she couldn't mask the sympathy in her voice.

Carefully, Kyle placed the necklace back in its box, then tucked it inside his bedside drawer. Scrambling to his feet, he followed Mrs. Sanders out the door and into the carpeted hallway.

He pressed the square crystal button of the elevator just as Mrs. Sanders came up beside him. Something shimmering on the floor caught his eye. He turned toward it and gasped. "Look!" he exclaimed, gazing around him in wonder. The sun streamed through the aquarium behind the elevator, casting blue and white dancing lights along the walls and carpet, making the hallway look like it was underwater.

"Oh, wow," Mrs. Sanders breathed. "It really is spectacular, but shouldn't we get to the lobby?" She placed her arm on Kyle's shoulder.

He stiffened, and he felt her hand lift before stepping onto the elevator. Kyle joined her, then continued to gaze at the shafts of light floating across the rocks and coral lining the large aquarium. He continued to watch the fish darting under the shafts of light until the aquarium disappeared above them and then they descended into the lobby.

He blinked, gawking at the hundreds of people walking over to the fountain, sitting in the chairs, or just standing in groups on the shiny marble tiles, probably also waiting for the departure.

Next to a huge glass fireplace anchored into the floor, a large crowd was gathered by the biggest glass window Kyle had ever seen. *How in the world did I miss it earlier?* he wondered as he stared at it in awe.

The elevator clicked into place and the doors slid open. Kyle and Mrs. Sanders stepped out onto the wooden walkway, and he was instantly aware of the loud buzzing sound of a lobby filled with chattering people. He followed Mrs. Sanders up the long walkway, his throat tightening. Mrs. Sanders turned left at the bridge, as they stepped onto the huge balcony overlooking the lobby.

"Looks like we're watching from up here," Mrs. Sanders said. "Well, look on the bright side. At least-"

"Attention, this is your captain speaking," a voice blared from behind them, and Mrs. Sanders gave an exasperated sigh. "Welcome aboard the *Dolphin Diamond*. The ship will be leaving in five minutes. Please feel free to walk around the ship, but I urge you to view the departure from either the Sapphire Deck, or through our state-of-the-art glass hull, designed by our incredible engineers. Also feel free to ask a crew member if you have any questions. Our crew is dedicated to making sure this cruise is one not easily forgotten. After the departure there will be a short orientation in the atrium at eleven-thirty on safety, events, shows, and facilities, as well as a very interesting demonstration. Enjoy your cruise! We will soon be on our way."

"Hold on a minute." Kyle turned to look at Mrs. Sanders, recalling what the captain had said. "On our way to where?"

"I didn't tell you already?" she asked, surprised. "Wow, I guess I forgot in all the excitement. There aren't that many places you can go on an eight- day cruise. I'll let you try to guess."

"Mom..." Kyle complained, then saw her playful expression. "Uh..." He thought for a moment, knowing it was useless to plead with her. "The Bahamas?"

"Nope, guess again." Mrs. Sanders smirked.

"Can't you just tell me?" He was sure that she was enjoying this.

"I'll give you a hint. Where the land meets the sea, and the sky meets a—"

Suddenly, the roar of a foghorn erupted into the lobby, and everyone stopped talking. The blast lasted a few seconds, then was replaced by silence before an excited buzzing flared up again.

Mrs. Sanders tried to say more, but Kyle could barely hear her. It seemed as if everyone was trying to talk over everyone else.

"Attention, all passengers," a voice called from the hidden speaker. The lobby quieted down a bit as some people stopped to hear the announcement. "That foghorn you just heard was the signal that the ship is about to depart."

The lobby erupted into noise again.

"Just tell me where we're going." Kyle had to almost shout to hear himself.

"Later," Mrs. Sanders shouted back.

Sighing, Kyle looked at the huge expanse of water running alongside the terminal and then at the horizon. What would it be like out there, surrounded by endless ocean? He suddenly longed to be out on the deck. The air in here was dry and cool, and although it felt nice, he would much rather be out with the hot, fresh air on his face.

"Do you think there's enough time to go up to the Sapphire Deck?" Kyle asked, turning toward Mrs. Sanders and raising his voice to be heard over the crowd.

"Well, I think eight days is enough time," Mrs. Sanders replied, grinning.

"I mean *before* we leave." Kyle couldn't help smiling as he rolled his eyes.

"Well..." Mrs. Sanders was interrupted by the crackling of the speakers again.

"Greetings, passengers, and welcome aboard the *Dolphin Diamond*! We are just about to leave port, but first, a quick announcement. For our guests' convenience, each room has been assigned an assistant who will be available to answer questions, point you to places, or serve you in any way they can. Well, here we go!"

Three short blasts burst from above them and the dock slowly inched away from the window.

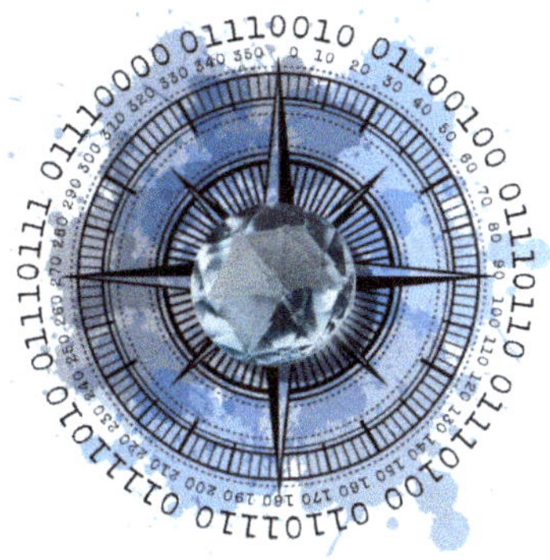

4

KYLE GRIPPED THE RAILING tighter, staring at the dock slipping further and further away, leaving a trail of white foam in its wake. It felt like a hundred butterflies were fluttering around in his stomach as the crowd erupted into cheers. He was on the ocean. He took a deep breath and squeezed his eyes shut. Mrs. Sanders was right. It wouldn't be like last time. This boat was a city, so there was no way it could sink.

"See? That wasn't so bad?" Mrs. Sanders said, as if reading his mind. "We're officially on our way to Marathon!"

Kyle turned to her, furrowing his brows. "Marathon?"

Mrs. Sanders gave him a sheepish smile. "Whoops. I *did* say that, didn't I? Marathon, Florida. It's a lower key near the Bahamas, right outside the Everglades. Along with being a tourist hub, it also has some pretty interesting attractions."

He decided not to ask her what the attractions were, partly because he kind of wanted them to be a surprise, and partly because she was giving him her mysterious grin again. "So what do we do now?" he asked instead. The crowd was already dispersing, and a huge group was heading toward the stairs to the balcony. Mrs. Sanders seemed to notice that too.

"Maybe we could head to the aft deck. We should still be able to see the mainland if we hurry." She turned around and strode down the bridge toward a glass elevator. Kyle ran to keep up as the group started up the stairs toward them. Making it to the elevator just before the group, he hit the button for the top floor. As soon as the doors closed, he let out a breath. He felt kind of bad for making everyone else wait for the next elevator, but he figured it was better than being squashed.

He found himself leaning against the glass, suddenly realizing how exhausting the morning had been. The day was just starting, and he was already tired, but he didn't really care. For the first time since he could remember, the empty place inside him was filled with happiness. He knew it wouldn't last long, but at least for a moment it felt nice.

They emerged into the clear sky, and Kyle looked up just in time to be blinded by the light reflecting off a huge slanting window high above them. He closed his eyes, then blinked into the brightness. When his vision cleared, he found he was staring at a sprawling deck with a brown shack in the middle, surrounded by umbrellas, tables, and chairs.

"Whew," Mrs. Sanders said, stepping out of the elevator just as the doors opened. Kyle followed her, and was hit by a blanket of hot humid sea air.

"Looks like we still have a ways to walk." She sighed. "Oh, well, come on!" She started briskly toward the stairs on the other side of the deck, and Kyle had to jog to keep up. Mrs. Sanders liked to get things done quickly no matter what they were, especially when it came to walking.

He was out of breath by the time they emerged on the Sapphire deck. A giant silver half-dome now curved away from them, glinting in the sunlight.

"Maybe—we could rest a little," Kyle said between gasps.

"You really need to build up your stamina," Mrs. Sanders put on a show of looking annoyed.

Suddenly, a voice boomed out of speakers somewhere behind them. "Attention, all passengers! Now that we're on our way, we invite you to join us for our presentation! It will be starting in fifteen minutes. We ask that you make your way over to the theater on the Sapphire deck, where our crew will assist you. Thank you for sailing on the *Dolphin Diamond* and we hope you have an amazing week!"

As the announcement ended, an adventurous tune struck up.

"I guess we're lucky." Mrs. Sanders chuckled. Kyle turned around to see what she meant, and his eyes went wide. To their left, the huge silver screen arched like a towering wave, with blue chairs clustered inside, as if they were riding the wave toward a giant stage with a white wall behind it.

"Looks like we've found the theater."

A few directions and two wrong turns later, they stepped out onto a carpeted balcony. Loud chatter filled Kyle's ears.

"This is pretty spectacular," Mrs. Sanders said, surveying the light-blue platform.

Kyle walked over to the edge of the balcony, grabbing onto the copper balustrade as he looked down at the tan walkway far below, leading to the edge of a pool mostly blocked by the huge white screen in front of them.

"It's pretty amazing. A city on the ocean," Mrs. Sanders mused from next to him.

Kyle jumped, spinning around. Why couldn't she clear her throat or something to let him know she was there?

"Sorry." Mrs. Sanders held up her hands, though her mouth curved up in an amused smile. "Beautiful, isn't it. Nothing but the ocean for hundreds of miles."

Looking back to the ocean, he thought about what must be out there under the waves. Where were the wild dolphins that his mother had worked with? Maybe they had migrated down to Florida and were below them right now. The thought of them being so close, but yet so far away, made his heart ache.

"…Thank you for sailing on the *Dolphin Diamond*, and enjoy the presentation!" Kyle realized he had been tuning out the speaker. He made his way back to his seat and sat down just as the adventurous music came to an end.

"Ladies and gentlemen." A young woman with brown hair and a ruffled purple T-shirt was standing near the front of the stage, holding a microphone. "Welcome to the fourth Emerald Seas presentation. As you can see by the timer behind me" —the young lady smiled, pointing to the screen— "we will be starting in about three minutes. If you need to use the restroom, you should do that now, though you will miss the introduction; so if you can, please wait until *after* the presentation. My name is Elizabeth Quigley, and I'm the main speaker onboard the *Dolphin Diamond*. And now, what we've all been waiting for: the Emerald Seas presentation!"

At this, the crowd around him erupted into cheers and applause, this time so loud he had to plug his ears.

"Thank you!" Elizabeth cried, smiling. "Now let's begin. We will start with our Safety and Evacuation Plan."

As she said this, the camera zoomed in on the ship, showing the top deck, while big glowing red letters appeared: *Safety and Evacuation.*

As Elizabeth droned on and on about where to meet up in case of an emergency and how the lifeboats worked, Kyle couldn't keep his mind from wandering back to the day he had met his mother's favorite dolphin.

"See, Kyle, you pet him like this." Kyle's mom slid her hand over Dusky's skin and let it slide off before it reached the scar on his dorsal fin. Kyle's own chubby hands awkwardly slid along Dusky's back, and he smiled when he felt the rubbery skin under his fingers. Dusky suddenly dove, disappearing for a second before surfacing again and letting out a series of clicks.

"What's he sayin'?"

"I don't really know," she replied, a strained look appearing on her face, "but I think he likes you."

He blinked as the memory faded. He had only been six then. Was Dusky even still alive?

Kyle glanced down at the carpet, and tears of homesickness filled his eyes.

"Kyle? Is something wrong?" Mrs. Sanders' voice startled him, and he looked up, then quickly glanced away, realizing she had seen his tears.

"I know you miss your old home," she continued, turning toward him. "You don't have to hide it from me."

He turned away, and Mrs. Sanders sighed. The screen in front of them erupted into white crystal words spelling out *The Emerald Seas*. A wind whipped around his head and all thoughts of his past blew away.

"Yes, ladies and gentlemen, this is the first outdoor 4-D theater ever to be put on a cruise ship!" Elizabeth exclaimed, "If you look to your right, you'll find a pair of 3-D glasses docked into the armrest. Just press the power button and put them on, and the screen will turn 3-D in a few seconds."

Excitedly, he slid on the slightly bulky glasses, then waited.

"Okay," Elizabeth said after a pause. "Since everyone is now settled, let the show begin!"

The letters on-screen faded, and a view of the cruise ship sailing on an endless ocean appeared.

A breeze brushed his hair, and he could smell the ocean's salty air, although it probably wasn't part of the effects. As the camera zoomed down and slammed into the water, the screen filled with a view of the ocean from below and a cool mist drifted over him.

"And, of course, the stars of the show: the dolphins!"

The air was filled with clicks and whistles as two Atlantic spotted dolphins appeared from the fog and swam toward the screen. One of them suddenly burst through, and Elizabeth ducked to avoid it, making the audience laugh.

"These are Atlantic spotted dolphins, one of the more common dolphins in the keys and Bahamas."

Kyle caught his breath. *It looks so real!*

"Atlantic spotted dolphins are known for their, well, spots. When they're first born, they're perfectly gray."

A light-gray dolphin calf burst onstage and swam enthusiastically around one of the other dolphins.

Kyle couldn't tear his eyes away from the dolphins as Elizabeth continued to talk about their behavior and traits. It was as if they were actually swimming around in the air. The rest of the presentation flew by in a flurry of bubbles, dolphins, and facts, such as where they would be seen during the cruise. It seemed too soon when the dolphins swam back into the screen and Elizabeth announced, "And now, to explore the *Dolphin Diamond*! But not on screen, of course. The presentation has ended, but take heart. *Your* adventure has just begun!"

As the screen zoomed back over the ocean, she performed a dramatic bow. The audience erupted into applause, and Elizabeth bowed again, then headed down the steps of the stage and disappeared below the crowd.

5

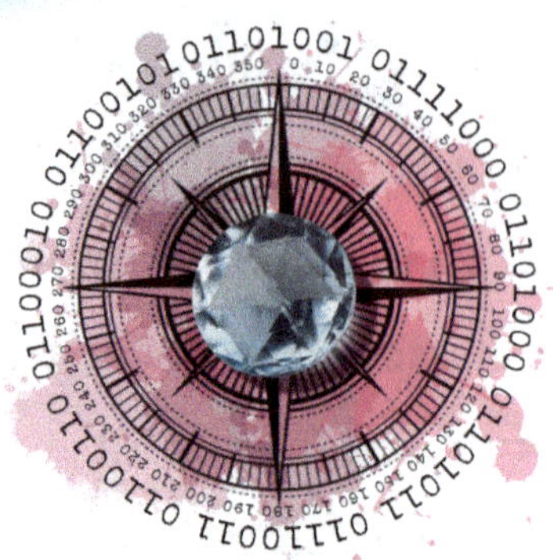

R IGHT NOW WOULD BE *the perfect time for a swim,* Kyle thought, imagining the cool water, which somehow made the heat feel worse. He glanced at the small shadow the thatched roof cast just in front of the window of Bravo's Bistro, then at the long line in front of them. Why couldn't they have built an overhang?

"Well, while we're waiting, what would you like for lunch?" Mrs. Sanders asked.

Kyle looked through the menu hanging on the wall of the hut. All of the food sounded delicious. The peach waffles with mango sauce made his mouth water, though the blueberry muffins seemed equally delicious. Maybe he could try whatever made that corn smell coming from the restaurant. He might also like a mango smoothie. *Or maybe a mango-lime smoothie,* he thought as he caught the words, "Mix two flavors for the price of one!" *And definitely some ice cream.*

He weighed all the options, then caught a delicious scent of sweet bread and mango. "Definitely the waffles."

Mrs. Sanders sighed. "I honestly have no idea what to get, myself! What do you think?" She turned to him, smiling.

"Maybe you could get the same thing?" Kyle said uncertainly, and his cheeks started to warm. It seemed weird giving advice to Mrs. Sanders, yet it was probably something a normal boy would do.

"That sounds like a plan," Mrs. Sanders agreed, stepping up to the counter as the person in front of them left. "I'd like four peach waffles with hot mango sauce please," she said to the man behind the window.

"Four Flamangos!" he shouted into the kitchen. Then, in almost the same breath he asked, "Would you like a drink or ice cream with that?"

"Whoops! I forgot about the ice creams. Kyle, which flavor would you like?"

Kyle looked up at the menu, and one flavor caught his eye. "I'll have apple cider," he announced, a wave of déjà vu coming over him.

"Two apple cider ice creams please," Mrs. Sanders said as the man placed a paper package on the counter.

"All right, just scan your wristband here." He pointed to a white, gem shaped reader on the counter. Mrs. Sanders scanned her wristband, and with a click, the gem glowed green.

"You're all set. Well bring your food to you shortly," the man said, already turning to the next person.

Mrs. Sanders pulled Kyle along behind her as they headed out of the line.

Kyle looked around at the tables. Half of them were already filled with people chatting and eating. Apprehensively, he followed Mrs. Sanders over to a free table. He scooted onto the sun-warmed wood, grateful for the shade of the umbrella.

Finally, a man brought them two steaming plates of waffles drizzled with light mango syrup, and a white carton with handles. Kyle bit into the warm fruity bread, savoring the taste, forgetting about the people around him. Apparently, Mrs. Sanders also loved it, as her eyes got huge and her eyebrows went up.

As Kyle started on his second waffle, he noticed one family at another table bow their heads as one of the boys started praying. Kyle didn't know why, but he felt a little guilty about not praying for his food. He had never eaten without praying before he lost his parents. Praying didn't really matter now though. It wasn't as if God listened to him anyway.

"You're full already?" Mrs. Sanders asked suddenly, looking at Kyle's untouched waffle.

She still had half a waffle in her hand, but he decided not to point that out.

"No. I was just thinking." He bit into the next waffle before Mrs. Sanders could grill him any further.

"Well, I hope the ice cream isn't melted," Mrs. Sanders spoke up, opening the carton, which was surprisingly thick and bendable, to find two cones of pale orange ice cream inside, still completely frozen.

"Now that's a good idea," she said. "An insulated carton."

Kyle grinned as he took out one of the chilly cones and caught the delicious apple smell, and he suddenly remembered why the ice cream seemed so familiar.

"Oh look, they have a new flavor," Kyle's mother commented, motioning him over to one of the little bowls which held two scoops of white ice cream streaked with pale yellow. "What's this one?" she asked the clerk behind the counter.

"That'd be our new coconut pineapple ice cream," the clerk said, maintaining her bored expression.

Little Kyle stepped away from that bowl quickly, and walked down the row of flavors until he found his favorite one, peach apple. "I'll have this one," he said, smiling up at the lady.

Her hard gaze softened. "Sure thing, Kyle, and you?" she asked, turning to Kyle's mother.

"I think I'll try the new one," Kyle's mother responded, twirling her long dark-brown hair.

"Two scoops of fruit orchard and two scoops of coconut surprise coming up," said the lady before walking into the kitchen.

Kyle suddenly turned and hugged his surprised mother.

"What was that for?" she asked.

"For taking me out to ice cream for no reason," he replied, smiling up at her.

"Hold on, I didn't take you out for no reason. You completely filled out your chore chart."

"Yeah, but I didn't know what the prize was," he cried happily, unable to stop the grin that spread over his face.

"Kyle, are you all right?"

He jerked from his memory to find Mrs. Sanders watching him and the melting cone with concern.

"I-I'm fine," he stuttered, the world starting to spin. He took a deep breath to steady himself.

"Kyle, are you *sure* you're alright?" Her voice filled with worry as she gazed at him. "Maybe—"

"No, I was just...remembering an ice cream place I went to with my mother." Longing stabbed through Kyle, and he looked down at the ice cream, his chest suddenly heavy.

"Oh, Kyle, I'm sorry..." Mrs. Sanders' usual carefree face filled with sympathy, which made him want to cry even more.

He tried to choke down the tears, but they came anyway. "Why did God take away my family?" he asked before he could stop himself.

Mrs. Sanders seemed startled for a second, but then regained herself. "Maybe He was testing you," she said uncomfortably, still looking him in the eyes.

Kyle felt his eyes flash. Why would she say something like that? God wouldn't kill his parents just to test him.

Looking down at his ice cream, he suddenly wanted to throw what was left of it at Mrs. Sanders. Instead, though, he put it back in the container. Why was he still angry after two years? Shouldn't he have just forgotten about it by now? Maybe Mrs. Sanders *was* right. Maybe God was testing him. Maybe God didn't care about Kyle's parents. Maybe God didn't even care about him at all. Kyle looked up from the table to find that Mrs. Sanders had already cleared away the container and was looking at him with a pained expression.

Guilt filled him, and he took a deep breath and closed his eyes, letting the cold ache take the place of his anger. A moment later, he felt an arm drape around his shoulder, and he tensed.

"Maybe God let your parents die to give me a wonderful son when I had just lost my own."

Kyle looked up, stunned, to see Mrs. Sanders' face was creased and her lips pressed together to stop herself from crying.

"You had a son?" He knew she had lost somebody right before she'd adopted him, but he always thought it had been her husband.

"Yes." Mrs. Sanders seemed to relax a bit. "His name was Tommy, and he was incredible. He was always going on adventures, though he never once got himself hurt on any of them. He loved baseball." She wiped her eyes, shaking her head. "One of the worst things about him was his ability to get into anything. I once found him on the top shelf of a bookcase, reading about codes, when he was three! I don't even know how he got up there!" She laughed at this, and Kyle couldn't help smiling even though he still felt like a ball of lead was in his stomach.

Someone cleared their throat, startling both of them. Kyle turned to see the man who had been behind the counter now standing above them.

"If you wouldn't mind..." The man smiled awkwardly. Mrs. Sanders looked startled, then stood up again and stepped out of the way as a man in a burgundy suit and a woman in a yellow dress walked past.

"Why don't we go back to our cabin and get settled, then we can figure out what to do from there," Mrs. Sanders said, putting on a smile as they walked between the tables.

Kyle smiled back, surprising himself. Maybe Mrs. Sanders wasn't his mother, but maybe she could at least be his mom.

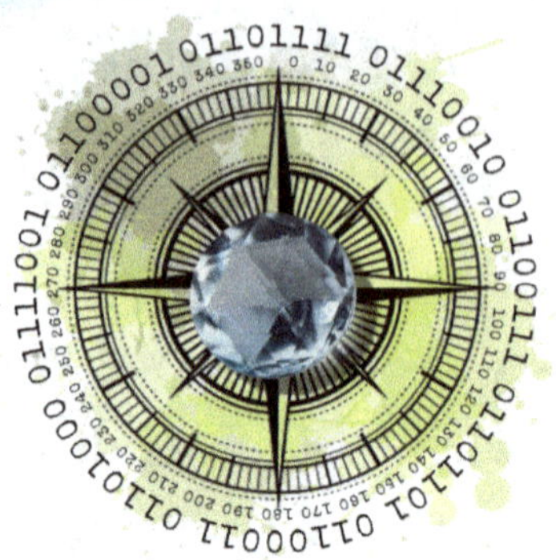

"So, Kyle." Mrs. Sanders' voice came from the other side of the bed, where she was busy reorganizing the clothes in her bedside drawer. "We still have daylight to burn. Do you have anything in mind you want to do?"

"How about swimming?" Kyle asked.

Mrs. Sanders grinned and slowly shook her head. "Honestly, why did I even ask?"

Kyle's face grew warm and he looked down at the deep maroon carpet, though he couldn't help but smile.

"Why don't you go get your stuff and change, then we'll leave after I'm done unpacking."

"Sure!" He spun around and walked over to the dark-brown cabinet. Opening the doors, he scanned the not-so-neat stack of clothes for his swimsuit. He spotted it lying under his pajamas, and yanked it out, then tossed it on the bed. Turning back to the closet, he found his goggles, towel, and travel bag and threw those on top of his swimsuit.

After he had changed, Kyle came out of the bathroom, clutching his goggles. He almost walked into Mrs. Sanders, who was waiting in front of the door, still in the same clothes.

"All right! Let's hit the deck!" Mrs. Sanders turned around and stepped into the hallway, ignoring the confusion that must have been on his face. *Maybe she's going to just watch.* Kyle followed her as she started off down the hallway toward the elevator. He raced ahead and pressed the crystal button before she could. A few moments later, the elevator emerged from below with three people aboard. Kyle couldn't help but smile as a little boy stared at the lemon shark swimming around a big orange fish.

The elevator came to a stop and the doors opened. Kyle and Mrs. Sanders stepped inside and they rose up and past the aquarium. As soon as it was gone the little boy, who seemed to be around two, looked up at one of the ladies.

"It gone," he said, making Kyle smile.

"Yes, but it'll still be there when we go down." The oldest woman replied, smiling down at the boy.

Kyle turned away as a breeze of warm humid sea air drifted into the elevator, hoping no one could see the tears he quickly blinked away. It felt like so long ago that he'd been the boy's age staring at a shark at the aquarium holding his mother's hand.

"Well, this is where we get off," said the younger lady, who looked like a college student. Kyle shook his head as the group hurried out of the elevator.

"I guess this is where we get off, too," Mrs. Sanders said, grinning at Kyle as she led him out of the elevator and over toward the staircase. Reaching the bottom of the stairs, she turned to him.

"I was thinking of heading to the garden area downstairs. Will you be fine if I drop you off here?"

Kyle stared at Mrs. Sanders for a moment, wondering if she was joking, though the look on her face made him realize she wasn't.

"It's okay, Kyle. I can stay with you. I can always see the garden later," she said, running a hand through Kyle's hair.

Kyle tensed and almost pulled away, but he found he couldn't move. It had been two years since the accident. Why couldn't he accept that Mrs. Sanders was his mom? *Because she's not,* he thought fiercely. Still, it felt oddly nice. *No.* He stepped away, barely realizing why he was doing it. He shook his head.

"No. I'll be fine," he said quickly, forcing himself not to look away.

Mrs. Sanders searched his face for a long moment, then slowly nodded. "Okay. I'll come get you in an hour. Just don't do anything stupid." She hesitated, then turned away and headed for the elevator.

He watched as she pressed the button and the doors closed. He stood there, alone, as the elevator descended; then disappeared. For the first time since he had lost his parent's Mrs. Sanders had left him alone. *I should feel scared, right?* All he felt, though, was a weight lifted off him. He was free.

Kyle smiled, turning and running up the glass steps. He swallowed as he caught sight of the huge ocean stretching into the distance all around, and for a moment, he wished his adoptive mom were here, telling him it was okay. He shook his head. He didn't need her. Shoving his fear down, he started down the path.

As soon as he caught sight of the sparkling water, all the fear disappeared, and he broke into a run. Bursting out of the walkway and onto a large open area, he immediately noticed the people. Most of them were clustered around the shallow end, though there were quite a few in the deep end and even a few on the island in the middle.

He slowed down as he scanned the pool for the place with the fewest people, and his attention was drawn to a girl in a light-blue T-shirt and tan shorts, sitting alone at the deep end.

He started to head over there, then stopped, suddenly recognizing her long, dirty-blonde hair. It was the same girl who had been sitting beside him in the waiting area. His heart started to beat faster. The girl—Ocean, he suddenly remembered—was sitting in the only place that wasn't crowded, which of course was exactly where he was heading.

Slowly, he made his way toward her, trying not to look her way. Maybe she wouldn't notice if he slipped by. His muscles tensed as he came beside her and started taking off his shoes, focusing on not glancing at her leg—at least, where her leg should have been.

Just as he was about to lower himself into the pool though, a girl in a black swimsuit with pink sides emerged from the water next to him. He tensed again, but she didn't pay any attention to him, instead staring at...Ocean? Like a spring, Ocean recoiled as the swimsuit girl pulled herself onto the deck and headed for the changing rooms.

Ocean quickly looked back down at the water, not seeming to notice Kyle. Then, so fast he almost missed it, the swimsuit girl spun around and shoved Ocean, hard.

"That's for running away," she snarled.

His stomach tightened as Ocean lost her balance and toppled into the water. He stared at her shape underwater. A second later she burst up to the surface, coughing and struggling to stay afloat. *She can't swim*, he realized, dread growing in his stomach.

Searching frantically for a lifeguard, he saw the only two around were talking to a lady in the shallow area. They hadn't even noticed Ocean falling in. In fact, no one around him seemed to have noticed either with all the shouting and splashing. His heart began to beat faster as he frantically turned back to the girls, watching as the swimsuit girl slipped back into the water. He knew what would come next even before it happened. He had to do something. He couldn't let the bully get to Ocean. He took a deep breath, then let it out. Still, he hesitated. Every nerve in him was telling him to jump in and help her, but his legs wouldn't move.

Ocean's wide eyes met his and he swallowed, gave one last look at the lifeguards, then dove into the pool. The shockingly cold water engulfed him, and for a second, all he could feel was a sharp stinging, as water went up his throat and the pressure pushed on him from every side. He tried to turn upward, but his feet slipped through the water, and he realized he was still wearing his shoes. Something smacked his arm and he opened his eyes to see someone's leg heading toward his face.

He dodged, his brain desperately signaling to surface, and without thinking about it he slipped his shoes off and kicked upward.

His heart caught in his throat as a hand pushed his head down. He tried to swim the other way, but whoever was pushing him down grabbed his hair, and Kyle felt a sharp pain as it went taut. He tried to fight the panic as he squeezed the hand holding his hair, hard. Instantly the grip lessened. He jerked it free and bolted upwards, his lungs begging for air.

Kyle burst through the surface, gasping as he looked wildly around. It took a moment for him to find where he was as he looked at the island a few feet to his left. By now some of the people were looking his way. He hadn't had time to see if the lifeguards had noticed yet when he heard a weak gasp from behind him. He turned around to see Ocean still floating there, her face barely out of the water. His heart still pounded as he looked around frantically then plummeted when he saw how far away the lifeguards were.

Suddenly, he heard another gasp, and he looked back at the spot where Ocean had been.

Feeling his goggles on his neck, he slipped them on and dove underwater. As the world went from the noise-filled air to silent blue, he instantly saw Ocean, her clothes clinging to her, kicking feebly at the girl in the swimsuit.

He automatically surged toward the swimsuit girl's arm, hearing his heart pounding in his ears. He angled himself down, touched the floor of the pool, then shot himself at her. The girl jerked away, her eyes wide behind her goggles, before she let go of Ocean and ducked beneath him.

He momentarily lost sight of the pink swimsuit, and he spun around, seeing the bully too late to react. He felt the impact as she slammed into him, knocking the air out of his lungs in a flurry of bubbles. As she grabbed his wrists and forced them behind his back, Kyle jabbed his knees toward her, his lungs begging for air again.

The bully dodged to the other side, letting go of Kyle for a second. That was all he needed, and he desperately swam upwards. With one last stroke, he broke the surface. Gasping in air, he shut his eyes, then heard a shrill whistle pierce the air. Relief flooded him. Finally, the lifeguard had noticed. He looked in the direction it came from. One of the lifeguards was kneeling at the edge of the pool, scowling at him.

"You are in big trouble, sir."

His head spun for a minute before he realized she was talking to him.

"This pool is not for horseplay," she said, anger in her voice.

The words lodged themselves in Kyle's heart as he remembered the girl he had been trying to save. He scanned the water, then spotted Ocean lying on the edge of the pool, not moving.

"No, wait, I didn't—"

The lifeguard scoffed. "Don't even try that on me. I saw everything that happened."

No, you didn't! You were too busy talking. Kyle bit his lip to stop himself from arguing any more. He knew that nothing he said would make a difference. The lifeguard hadn't seen what had happened.

As soon as he reached the wall, Kyle climbed up out of the water, not wanting to get into any more trouble. His heart leapt into his throat as he saw Ocean lying on the ground in a puddle of water, her now dark-blue T-shirt heaving. At least she was alive.

The lifeguard immediately knelt by Ocean's side, pressing her hand to the girl's neck. "Her pulse is still steady, and she doesn't seem to have inhaled any water," she said into a little radio clipped to her shoulder.

"Roger. I'll fill in for you so you can take them down to the clinic. Over," a young Australian voice crackled through.

"Roger that. I'll take them below. Over and out." The lifeguard released the radio, then turned to Kyle. "Sir, what's your name?"

Kyle glared at the lifeguard, wondering if he should tell her, though it was obvious from her stare that he couldn't stay silent.

"It's Kyle," he said shortly, looking down at his feet to avoid the unrelenting glare.

"And what are your parents' name? I'm going to have to call them."

"No, you won't," a young woman's familiar voice said from behind him. He turned around to see the speaker from the presentation standing there, staring firmly at the lifeguard. "I saw what happened. If you have any complaints, they will be against me."

The lifeguard looked taken aback for a second, then she narrowed her eyes. "That would be against policy... Beth, isn't it?"

Before Elizabeth could respond, Ocean's arm stirred, then she opened her eyes, staring in confusion at the lifeguard, then at Kyle. Kyle held his breath, wondering if she had somehow gotten a concussion.

"Hey. You're going to be okay," the lifeguard said, turning back to the girl with a sudden caring expression.

He was stunned at how quickly her tone had changed.

"I can't..." Ocean trailed off, and she closed her eyes, swaying as she tried to sit up.

The lifeguard put her hands on Ocean's shoulders. "Hey, it's okay. It's over now." She had lost her commanding tone, and almost seemed like a mother.

The girl took a deep breath and closed her eyes, seeming to focus on breathing.

"That's good. Keep taking deep breaths. Now, for you." The lifeguard turned to Kyle, her lips forming a thin line. Her face turned into a scowl as she glanced at Beth. Kyle's face heated up. He knew what she was about to say, but all she said was, "I have to take her to the clinic and you're coming with us."

"He didn't do it," a soft but firm voice said. Startled, Kyle looked at Ocean.

"Young lady, I saw what happened. Don't think you're not in trouble too," the lifeguard said, turning to her.

"Her name's Brianna," Ocean continued, closing her eyes as she spoke, and Kyle noticed how pale her face was.

"Well then, if this *Brianna* was involved, where is she *now*?" The lifeguard's voice was edged in annoyance, and the only response was a group of girls breaking into laughter.

Where *was* the bully? Kyle looked back over to the pool, but she was gone. Why had she tried to drown them? He shivered to think of what would have happened if he hadn't jumped in. Would Ocean even still be alive?

When Ocean didn't reply, the lifeguard nodded smugly. "That's what I thought." She stared at Ocean with what Kyle guessed was the same stare she had used on him. "Can I ask what *your* parents' names are, miss?"

Ocean let her blonde hair fall onto her back as she tilted her head to look at the lifeguard.

"My *dad's* name is Paul," she said quietly, giving the lifeguard a penetrating stare that seemed to go right through her.

The lifeguard hesitated a second, not breaking eye contact. "Do you know where he is on the ship?" Her tone was soft again, which might have had something to do with Ocean's glare.

"He said he'd be in the garden, wherever that is." Ocean's voice was still low.

"Okay. We'll swing by there to let him know what's going on, then we'll take you to the clinic," the lifeguard said firmly, glancing at Ocean's prosthetic leg. "Can you walk?"

"Of course I can walk," Ocean replied, rolling to the side then shoving off with her good leg as she pushed herself shakily to her feet. She squeezed her eyes shut, and her leg gave out, sending her falling. In a blink of an eye, the lifeguard had her arm around her.

"I guess not," the lifeguard said. "Looks like I'll have to help you." She gave a reassuring smile.

Dripping wet, the three of them started slowly toward the double doors to the right of the pool. Kyle glanced back awkwardly at the woman smiling after him. Why had Elizabeth stood up for him? She didn't even *know* him. He shook the odd feeling out of his mind as the lifeguard freed one arm to push a pair of oak double doors open. They entered a small, brown, carpeted room with a crystal-raindrop chandelier, and Kyle was blasted by freezing air. Tensing at the sudden cold, he forced himself to walk forward. Glancing down the corridor, he could also just barely make out the back of a brown recliner down a wide hallway. He stiffened as a fresh frigid breeze blew against him, and silently followed the lifeguard to the elevator, waiting as she pressed the crystal button and the elevator doors opened.

"I think I can stand on my own now," Ocean said, and the lifeguard took her arm out from under Ocean's. Ocean looked tired, though she was able to keep her balance as the elevator started descending.

Kyle turned to look out through the glass, watching the maroon-carpeted corridor slide past as they descended through the floor and into a rainforest.

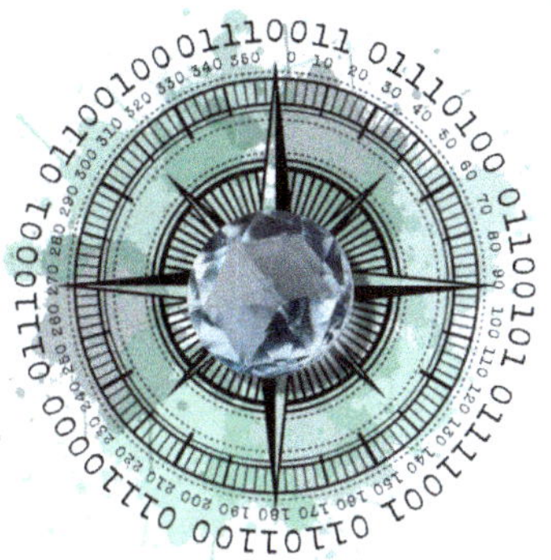

THE GLASS DOORS OF the elevator slid open, warm mist spilling inside and Kyle's body relaxed as he looked out into the steamy rainforest beyond. The trees rose up into the haze where the green fronds spread out over them, casting shadows on the dark wooden path.

"Welcome to the Diamond Gardens." The lifeguard's tone had changed, as though the beauty of the garden had softened even her for a moment. "Now," she said, her voice turning icy again, "let's find your parents."

As they stepped out of the elevator and started walking down the path, Kyle realized that not only did it *look* like a rainforest, but it also sounded like one. The jungle echoed with bird calls and the splattering of rain on the canopy. Somewhere nearby, he could hear running water and the sound of frogs croaking.

"Look over there!" Ocean suddenly exclaimed, pointing into a group of palm fronds.

Kyle followed her gaze, but he couldn't see anything out of the ordinary. Then, almost so fast he missed it, a flash of red and yellow rustled the leaves, and a bird leaped out of the tree and fluttered to another one. Kyle paused for a moment, gazing up as another one took flight on his left.

"Wow…" he marveled, turning around.

"Come on. We need to get a move on," the lifeguard said firmly, shattering the majesty of the place.

Reluctantly, Kyle followed. At least he wasn't in trouble any-more. Or at least he *hoped* he wasn't.

As the group turned a corner, he saw that the trees ended at a huge raised clearing bursting with tropical flowers. They emerged from the rainforest, and Kyle caught sight of Mrs. Sanders talking with a bearded man with gray hair. *Ocean's father?*

"Hey, there he is," Ocean said from behind, and then her footsteps suddenly stopped. Kyle looked back to see her biting her lip, a look of confusion on her face.

"Kyle?" He heard the familiar voice and turned his head to see Mrs. Sanders looking worriedly at him.

The gray-haired man—what had Ocean said his name was? Paul—also turned toward them, and his eyebrows rose in sur-prise.

"What are you doing here?" Paul narrowed his eyes. "Ocean! You're soaked!"

"I assume you're Kyle and Ocean's parents?" the lifeguard said, her voice dripping with annoyance.

"Yes. That's my daughter," Paul said. "However, he's her son, not mine." He motioned to Mrs. Sanders.

The lifeguard hesitated a moment, as if trying to figure out what to say next. "Yes. Well, I found both of them in the pool fighting with—" She paused, and Kyle's heart started pounding, his face instantly feeling hot.

Please don't say it was me, he pleaded.

"—Another girl," the lifeguard finished. Apparently she decided to take Ocean's word for it, and Kyle breathed a sigh of relief.

"*Ocean?*" Paul's question was directed at the girl, and Kyle could see the intense worry in his wrinkled forehead.

"Yes, sir," the lifeguard answered, when Ocean didn't respond. "I was going to take her to the clinic. I just wanted to stop by and let you know what's going on."

"Thank you, but I don't think it's necessary," he said, his eyes narrowing.

"I'm sorry, sir, but it's against protocol to send her back with you," the lifeguard said firmly. "She needs to see a doctor."

The man looked from Ocean to the lifeguard, then at Ocean again. He slowly nodded, sighing. "Okay. *I'll* take her."

The lifeguard seemed to consider it. Finally, she nodded curtly. "Thank you, sir," she said, seeming relieved that the whole thing was over. With that, she turned and headed away, the flopping sound of her footsteps fading into the trees.

Paul sighed deeply, and gave Ocean a stern, questioning look. Without warning, Ocean ran to him and buried her head in his chest, and Kyle felt the pang of loneliness jab into him even harder. His heart ached as he remembered how much he had loved his own father. How much he *still* loved him, Kyle thought fiercely, remembering the last time he had seen his father, running toward the helm of the *Emerald Wind* to try to save Kyle, before his own life had been taken.

"Kyle, are you okay?" Mrs. Sanders' voice came from beside him.

He snapped out of his thoughts and looked down at the tiled path, feeling just as cold as the gray pebbles.

"Yeah, I'm fine." He tried to sound upbeat. It came out as more of a choked squeak, though. Without warning, he buried himself in Mrs. Sanders' shirt as hot tears fell down his face. After a few minutes of standing there, Mrs. Sanders pulled away and knelt down in front of him.

"I'll always be here for you, Kyle."

Kyle felt another tear slide down his cheek as he saw the concern in Mrs. Sanders' eyes. He quickly wiped it away and turned toward the jungle, realizing that Ocean was probably watching him.

"Kyle..."

Kyle jumped at Ocean's voice, which was only a foot behind him. Spinning around, he saw her looking at him awkwardly, and his heart started beating faster as he glanced down at the shiny metal stretching from her foot to her knee.

"Thanks for saving me," she whispered, pulling him into a hug. Caught off guard, Kyle stared at Mrs. Sanders, who was finding it hard not to laugh. Finally, Ocean let go of him, and Kyle stepped away, his face burning.

Ocean grinned at him, twirling her dirty-blonde hair around her finger.

"My dad says you can come over any time you want to. We're in room A 96."

"Thanks," Kyle replied, taking a deep breath. Ocean wanted to become friends with him, and he almost couldn't believe it was happening. He couldn't remember ever having a friend. How would he know how to act? He looked away from her face, his eyes landing on the metal rod in her leg. *Does it hurt her to wear it?* His stomach churned at the thought, and he quickly glanced away.

"I know you hate going to the clinic," Paul put a hand on Ocean's shoulder, "but I told the lifeguard I would bring you, so let's get this over with." Without another word, he gently pushed her down the path back toward the elevator. Ocean's smile instantly disappeared.

A few steps away, her dad turned. "You're welcome to come along, if you want. I'm sure Ocean would be glad of the company."

Her cheeks grew red, and Kyle hesitated, glancing at Mrs. Sanders, who nodded, smiling. Biting his lip, he walked up beside Ocean, wondering what he could say to her. *Why doesn't she want to go to the clinic anyway?*

"I'm sure it won't be that bad. They'll just check your breathing and…" He trailed off as Ocean's father glanced a warning at him.

A long moment of silence followed, interrupted only by the shrieking birds and Mrs. Sanders and Paul's whispered conversation. Kyle couldn't decide which was worse. Finally, he couldn't take it anymore. He asked the first thing that popped into his head. "Have you seen the aquariums yet?"

Ocean looked startled, then turned to him, a spark in her eyes. "Aquariums?"

"Yeah." He smiled. Finally there was something she wanted to talk about. "There's an aquarium on the second deck that you can see from the elevator."

Ocean smiled shyly at him, then looked down at the wooden floor of the walkway.

"I guess you have to like the ocean, your name being Ocean and all." As soon as Kyle said that, Paul stiffened and glanced at Ocean, who looked away from both of them. *So much for trying to talk to her.* Why did talking have to be so complicated? Kyle decided to just give up as they stepped onto the marble floor of the lobby.

As they neared the glass elevator, he glanced back at Ocean, who looked like a cornered puppy. Her father seemed to notice, and he gave a long sigh.

"Ocean, I don't want to go any more than you do, but a promise is a promise." With that he hit the button and the elevator doors slid open. He had to basically drag her inside before the doors closed and they started rising.

Without knowing exactly why he did it, Kyle grabbed Ocean's hand, squeezing it in what he hoped was a comforting way. For a moment, she seemed to forget about where they were going as she smirked at him, then squeezed his hand, hard. He winced, pulling away quickly. He tried to ignore Mrs. Sanders' snort as he stared at the window, the fog disappearing to reveal a hallway he had seen outside his own room.

With a jolt, the elevator came to a stop and the doors opened. Ocean instinctively shrank back. Without thinking about it, Kyle gripped her hand again, and this time, she didn't try to kill it. Together, they headed into the hallway and toward the room with a huge red cross painted on it.

8

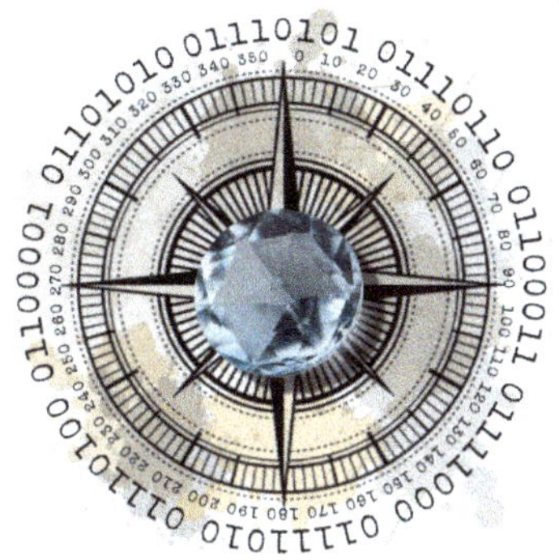

"Sᴏ ᴅᴏᴇsɴ'ᴛ ᴀᴘᴘᴇᴀʀ ᴛᴏ have inhaled any water," the nurse announced, taking off his gloves and placing them on the metal tray in the middle of the room. "It seems like she passed out from asphyxiation, though she checks out fine."

"Well, thank you," Ocean's father said, tight-lipped as he got up from the blue padded chair. "I appreciate your help."

Kyle was still shocked at how quickly Paul's tone had changed when they had entered the clinic. He was obviously hiding something. Ocean was sitting on the examination bed, looking down at the tiled floor, holding onto her father's hand with white knuckles.

The nurse looked like he was about to say something, then stopped himself, and instead, he sighed.

"I guess I can't hold you any longer. If she starts developing anything out of the ordinary, bring her back, even if it looks like a cold." He opened the door and Paul walked out into the hallway, followed by Ocean, Mrs. Sanders, and Kyle.

Without another word, the nurse stepped out of the room, closing the door behind him, and led the group to the waiting room at the entrance of the clinic.

"Have a nice day," he said, putting on a forced smile before disappearing into the back of the clinic.

"Seems like everyone on this ship has been having a rough day," Mrs. Sanders commented, frowning at the door the nurse had disappeared through.

Kyle had to agree with that. Boarding day must be tough on them, getting everything ready for a week. He followed the others through the glass door and into the tiled hallway, where a jewelry shop stood opposite them.

Ocean suddenly tensed up as her father came alongside her, and Kyle blinked in confusion. She had just been holding Paul's hand in the clinic and now she was tensing when he approached her? It didn't make sense. She wasn't even looking at him. Kyle followed her gaze. Behind a glass door, he could see two pools, and in the largest one, the girl in the pink and black swimsuit was swimming laps.

Ocean's dad seemed to notice her too.

"You know what, that shop looks interesting. Why don't we stop in and have a look?"

Without waiting for a response, he quickly led a confused Mrs. Sanders and the others across the hallway into the little jewelry shop with a crystal *C* stenciled into the window.

"Oh, hello there," a thick British accent greeted them from behind the wooden desk. A second later, a man with slicked-back brown hair emerged smiling, holding a box. "Welcome to Craft Crystal Jewelry. I'll be right here if you need assistance." He then turned, humming a tune Kyle didn't recognize.

"Well, I guess not *all* the crew members are grouchy," Mrs. Sanders whispered to Kyle, who tried to hide a grin as he watched the clerk taking jewelry out of the box, occasionally trying a piece on, then putting it in the display case. One of the objects caught Kyle's eye, and he gasped when he recognized it.

"Is something wrong?" the clerk asked, turning to face him. He still held a necklace, which carried a perfectly carved wooden leaping dolphin.

"Where did you get that?" Kyle's tone sounded more demanding than he had intended, but the clerk didn't seem to notice.

"Oh, well, it's actually a very odd story." The man winked at Kyle. "This necklace was found inside a sunken ship in the Caribbean. A team of divers were going through the wreckage, when they found a small, intricately carved wooden box, and even though the ship was rotten, somehow this box looked brand new. Thinking they had found a valuable treasure, they surfaced and tried to open the box, but it was locked. Eventually, they had to pry the lid off, which, sadly, destroyed the box." The man sighed. "Boy, were they disappointed when they saw the treasure wasn't gold, but this dolphin necklace." He motioned toward it. "They decided that they should keep the treasure and gave it to the diver who had found it. That diver just happened to be me."

"Wow, it's pretty."

Kyle started, realizing that Ocean had come up beside him.

"Yes, it is, though it's only for display purposes, since it's one of a kind."

Ocean's face fell.

"I'll tell you what, though. If you can find one exactly like it, I'll give it to you for free."

Kyle tensed as the man looked at him.

"Well, I'd better tidy up my shop before the mobs come tomorrow," the clerk said cheerily as he walked back to the desk and continued unpacking.

"I guess I should shop now, then," Mrs. Sanders commented from near a necklace stand.

As she started looking through the necklaces, Kyle walked over to the glass case where the clerk had put the dolphin necklace on display. Studying it closer, he saw how perfect it looked. Each fin was the same size, and the body curved majestically to a perfect fluke at the bottom. It was too flawless to be handmade, so maybe it was just a coincidence that it looked identical to the one he had.

"Pretty, isn't it?" the man said from above him, making Kyle's head snap up.

"Yeah, it looks so perfect." Kyle cringed, hoping his hint didn't sound as obvious to the clerk as it did to him.

"Ah, yes. Carved by the hand of a master woodsmith."

"Wait, how would *you* know?" Ocean asked suspiciously, startling Kyle.

"Oh, I—" The man paused. "It was just an educated guess. Seeing that it's wood and all, it only makes sense."

Ocean grinned as she gave the clerk a penetrating stare then turned around and walked over to where her dad was standing, looking like he was about to burst out laughing. Kyle turned to see what Paul was looking at and couldn't hold back a smile. Mrs. Sanders was trying on a huge emerald teardrop necklace that made her look like a peacock.

"My," the clerk announced from behind the counter, trying to keep a straight face. "You really look like Cleopatra in that."

Kyle watched in surprise as Mrs. Sanders' face flushed.

"Thank you, but we really need to get going." She quickly took the necklace off and put it back on the stand, then hurried toward the door. "Come on, Kyle."

"Have a nice day," the clerk called after them.

Without replying, Mrs. Sanders stalked out of the shop. Kyle followed, confused.

"Did I really look like Cleopatra?" she asked, stopping to look at him.

Kyle scrunched up his face, wondering what he should say that wouldn't sound bad.

"You looked more like a peacock," he admitted, immediately regretting saying it as his cheeks burned.

Mrs. Sanders' gaze softened a little. "I never did like jewelry that much, and I certainly do not like that clerk."

Kyle had to agree on that. There was something off about the man.

"We're going back to our cabin. If you want, you can come with us," Ocean said from behind Kyle.

Kyle shook his thoughts away, turning to Ocean in surprise.

Paul turned to Mrs. Sanders. "How would you like to meet up together again at the Diamond Diner for dinner?"

"Well..." Mrs. Sanders said, deep in thought. "I don't see why not. How about you, Kyle?"

Kyle looked from Mrs. Sanders to Ocean, then to Paul. An odd feeling flowed through him. It was kind of nice. He had never been invited to someone's home before, although Ocean's cabin didn't really count as a home. He swallowed, fear starting to creep into his mind. If he didn't decide soon, he would never be able to.

"Sure..." The word came out more hesitant than he had meant, though Ocean didn't seem to notice as she broke into a grin.

"Great! I'm sure you'll love it," she said, the spark in her eyes growing brighter. With that, she spun around and nearly toppled over as the shoe attached to her prosthetic snagged on the carpet. She quickly caught herself, putting her weight on her other foot, then grinning back at Kyle.

"Well, come on," she said, as if nothing had happened. With that she turned and hurried after her dad.

Kyle started after them, Mrs. Sanders right behind him. He tried to hide his uneasiness, but apparently he didn't do a very good job.

"Don't worry, Kyle," she whispered to him. "You and Ocean seem to get along really well. I'm sure you two will have a great time. And who knows. Maybe she'll ask you out." She winked.

That was all he needed. Cheeks burning, he hurried to catch up with Ocean and her father, leaving Mrs. Sanders behind. Closing his eyes, he took a deep breath, trying to get rid of the uneasiness in his chest. It was too late to turn back now.

"Guess you're eager to see our famous suite," Paul said.

Kyle swallowed, then nodded, feeling his throat tighten. He didn't know how to reply. Ocean dropped back to walk beside Kyle, and he realized that he was trying to stay behind them and not be noticed, like he always did in groups.

"So, what do you like to do?" Ocean asked, smiling at him.

"I guess..." Kyle trailed off, tilting his head. How could such a simple question be so hard? "I like to swim." Suddenly, he regretted saying that, remembering what had happened in the pool. He expected Ocean to look away again, but instead she half-smiled.

"I used to," she responded quietly, her cheeks turning slightly pink, "but I..." She trailed off, glancing down at the thick metal rod below her knee.

He guessed that was why she couldn't swim anymore, and he felt a twinge of compassion for her.

"Is there anything else you like to do?" she asked, changing the topic.

Before Kyle could answer Ocean's question, though, her father spoke up. "All right, our room's just on the next deck."

Suddenly, Kyle remembered Mrs. Sanders. He looked back, but she was gone. *Okay, you can do this. You don't need her.* Kyle glanced up to see the double wooden doors that led out to the elevators. Ocean's father grabbed one of the doors and swung it open, and the three of them walked down the long corridor, until they reached the glass elevator with the aquarium behind it.

Noticing that his friend had suddenly stopped, Kyle glanced to his right to see her staring into the large tank, her eyes wide.

"She could be here for hours," Paul whispered, and Kyle caught a whiff of pine from the man's face.

"It's a lemon shark," Ocean breathed. Kyle looked up just in time to see the white underbelly of the shark as it spun around and darted away from them, headed toward the surface.

"Well, this is really interesting, but Ocean, wasn't there something we were showing Kyle?" Paul asked, raising his eyebrows.

Sighing, Ocean turned away from the aquariums and quickly headed into the elevator, then turned back to watch the fish as Kyle walked in next to her.

"Well, we're all aboard. Next stop, the City of Amber," Ocean's father announced as he punched the button for the third level, and the clear doors slid closed. The elevator started rising, and Kyle stared at the fish that were coming closer. Glancing at Ocean, he could see a distant look on her face. She didn't even seem to be watching the fish anymore.

With a slight jolt, the elevator came to a stop, and the doors opened. Fresh sea air streamed in, along with light that blinded Kyle.

"I don't think we're in Kansas anymore, Ocean," Paul announced, stepping out of the elevator. Out of the corner of his eye, Kyle saw Ocean roll her own eyes, though she was grinning.

"Come on. You're going to love it!" With that, she spun and headed out onto the deck, dodging around the tables of Bravo's bistro.

Kyle hurried to catch up with her, glancing behind him as Paul lagged behind. Turning back to Ocean, he was about to suggest they wait for her father, but the thought disappeared as he noticed that Ocean was heading off to the right, steering clear of the pool. Heart picking up speed, he scanned the water for any sign of a pink and black swimsuit, relaxing when he didn't see any.

Kyle turned his head just in time to see the staircase, and he dodged to the right, bumping into Ocean's shoulder. The impact threw her off balance, and before he knew what was happening, he had grabbed her arm. He froze, stiffening, though he resisted the urge to let go, instead pulling her back to her feet. His face burned as she gave him an odd look.

"Thanks," she said, glancing toward the water.

Luckily, Paul's voice broke the awkwardness.

"Come on, tigers, the suite's this way."

Kyle followed him to a set of double oak doors and into a maroon-carpeted hallway with fancy candelabras on the gold and cream patterned wall.

"Well, here it is," Ocean's father said, going up to one of the dark oak doors. "Suite A 96." Casually, he swiped his wrist over the lock. A click sounded, and he threw open the door.

Kyle almost gasped at the sight. The entire room looked like the ocean. The ceiling was an explosion of white ripples that gradually turned into blue at the sides, where it ran down the walls, fading into a navy. Set into the opposite wall was a huge window looking out onto a balcony and the ocean beyond.

As he stepped into the room, Kyle's feet sank into the soft tan carpet and the scent of flowers wafted past him. The layout was almost the opposite of Kyle's cabin. On the left, there were two huge beds with turquoise pillows and blankets,  and he wondered how anyone could sleep with so many pillows. As his gaze moved right, his mouth fell open.

Two giant dressers were placed up against the wall, each with mother-of-pearl knobs and dark, rustic wood. There was no way Ocean and her father had enough clothes to fill it up, Kyle thought, remembering his small stuffed dresser back in his room. He'd never imagined Ocean as being rich, but she had to be to get a cabin like this.

"So, do you like it?" Ocean asked from behind him.

Turning around, Kyle tried to hide his envy, though Ocean's eyes seemed to bore into his and it was clear she could see it.

"You can come over here any time you want," she offered, then she seemed to remember something, and looked at her father.

"You're welcome here any time," he confirmed. "Just ask first, okay?"

Swallowing, Kyle nodded, suddenly awkward. He was still trying to get used to the fact that he had a friend.

"So, now what do you want to do?" Ocean asked.

He blinked. What was there to do in a room on a cruise ship? *What do normal friends do?* "Do you have any movies?" He asked, noticing an enormous flat-screen TV, which hung on the wall facing the beds.

Ocean grinned walking over to a drawer under the TV. "We probably have enough to last us through the entire cruise."

Cautiously, Kyle followed, and in a few moments they were both digging through the seemingly endless rows of DVDs.

Kyle stopped at a disk that showed a picture of a coral reef. Carefully, he removed it. "This one looks interesting. 'Journey Under the Seas,'" he read, then tensed. "I mean... If you—"

"Sure," Ocean said, grinning. "I mean, I'm sure I've watched that one before, but I don't really remember it." She took the DVD from him and inserted it into the TV. A few seconds later, the documentary started, and Kyle was instantly caught up in the breathtaking shots of rays, dolphins, and sharks as the narrator talked about the life of each under the ocean. It seemed almost too soon when the narrator dramatically ended with, "And although one season has ended, a new one has begun, and with it comes the struggle of life under the seas."

Ocean sighed from next to Kyle. "You know what's the worst thing about documentaries?"

Kyle looked over to see her grinning. "When they end?" he guessed, and she looked at him, faking bewilderment.

"No. After the end, when they're over." She grinned at him when he gave her a confused look.

"She gets it from me," Paul said from the other bed, and Kyle jumped.

He had completely forgotten about Paul. Had he been there the entire time? A dense silence followed, and Kyle realized that they must be waiting for him to say something. A thought that had been in the back of his mind suddenly returned, and without really thinking about it, he blurted out, "If you're afraid of water, why do you like underwater documentaries?" He instantly regretted saying it when both Ocean and her father tensed.

Finally, Paul sighed. "It's a long story. Maybe I should—"

"No. I should."

Kyle looked back and forth between them, confused. Ocean took another deep breath.

"I don't remember why I became afraid of the water. My mom always took me to the beach, trying to teach me not to be afraid of it. Eventually, I was able to swim across the bay, but she never got me to swim underwater. I—" Ocean closed her eyes, and took another deep breath. "I just couldn't. Then, she disappeared." Ocean didn't say any more, and Kyle noticed a tear fall down her face. "Maybe if I had gone with her..." She stopped, looking at the wall.

A thousand questions flew through Kyle's mind. He had thought that she had stopped swimming because of her prosthetic. When did she get it? And what happened to her leg? Forcing these thoughts aside, he looked at Ocean's face, and something his mother had always said flashed through his mind.

"You can't stop something that's already passed," he said. Thinking of his mother made his throat start to tighten, and he glanced at the sandy-colored carpet.

"And, Ocean," Paul added, "if you had gone with her, you would have...I would have lost you, too."

A knock interrupted them, then another. Kyle watched Ocean's father cross the room and open the door. Mrs. Sanders stood in the shadowy maroon corridor, looking slightly awk-ward.

"Did I interrupt anything?" she asked, glancing at Kyle, then Ocean.

"No, not...really." Ocean's father smiled, motioning for her to come in.

Mrs. Sanders stepped into the room, gazing around her with awe.

"This is a really neat place you have," she commented, coming over to the bed where Kyle was sitting. "So, what have you two been up to?"

Kyle looked over at Ocean, who was biting her lip, looking uncomfortable.

"We watched a documentary. Then we just talked," he offered, feeling himself growing hot. *That's one way to put it.*

"Great." Mrs. Sanders smirked. "I was thinking we could go grab dinner? It's 4:30, so there shouldn't be too many people at the diner yet."

"We have no other plans," Paul said, motioning everyone toward the door. "Come on, Ocean, I don't know about you, but I could use some food."

Kyle glanced at Ocean, seeing a pained look on her face, and wondered what else she was hiding from him.

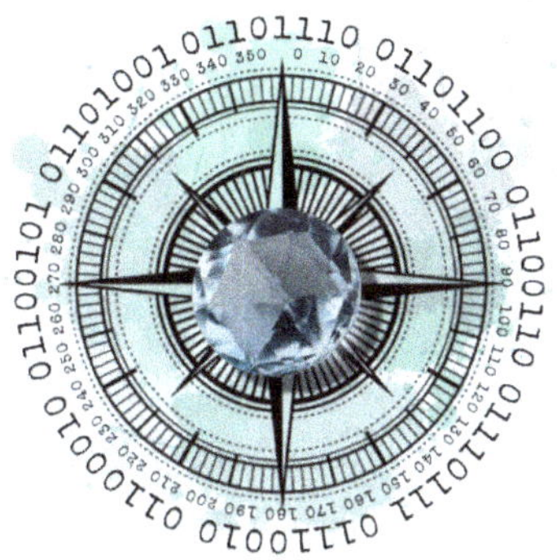

9

THE CLANKING OF DISHES filled the air as Kyle and the others stepped onto the dark wooden floor of the diner. Kyle looked around him at the delicate-looking chairs, tables, and shiny brown plush benches. The place was already crowded, and he couldn't make sense of the bustling waiters and the winding paths. Luckily, though, Mrs. Sanders didn't seem fazed as she took the lead.

As they approached their seats, Kyle spotted two girls staring at him, and he was just in time to see one of their faces before she looked down at her phone. His heart nearly stopped. It was the girl who had pushed Ocean into the pool. *Brianna.*

Suddenly, the hot anger he had felt at the pool came rushing back, and Kyle glanced down, focusing on the seat they were approaching, which happened to be the one across from the girl.

"You want to go back to the pool tonight?" The girl next to Brianna asked her as Kyle sat down next to Mrs. Sanders. The girl almost sounded nice, and Kyle wondered why she hung out with that bully.

"Sure," Brianna replied, "At least there won't be any lifeguards then. They're always watching you, trying to get you in trouble for something."

Heat flooded Kyle's face. Of course they would get you in trouble if you went around trying to drown kids.

"Uhh, Kyle, your menu is in front of you," Ocean said softly from beside him.

He looked down at his menu, pretending to read it as he heard the other girl talking.

"...that necklace looked amazing?"

"It actually looked pretty creepy. Dolphins are supposed to smile. That one just looked like it had eaten a bad fish."

Kyle cocked his head. *They've seen the necklace too.*

"And I don't think the guy's story was true. You don't find a dolphin necklace in a plane wreck in the jungle. He also said he had no idea what the plane's name was, so either he stole the necklace without telling the government, or he's lying."

Kyle couldn't keep back a grin, remembering the completely different story the clerk had told him.

"Kyle, what do you want?" Mrs. Sanders's voice cut through his thoughts.

His mind snapped back to their table, and he looked up to see a waiter waiting with a notepad and pencil, looking expectantly at him. Frantically, he glanced down at the menu, scanning the options, which all looked foreign, so he said the first one he recognized.

"I'd like a salmon omelette." He felt his face heating up, and he glanced at Mrs. Sanders, seeing her eyebrow go up.

"All right," the waiter announced, writing something down. "One plate of garlic tomato spaghetti, two bowls of chili, and a salmon omelette coming right up." With that, he turned and walked away.

"A salmon omelette. That's a first." Mrs. Sanders grinned. "Last time I checked, you would never try anything new."

"I guess I changed my mind," Kyle said, looking down at the table.

"If you don't like it, we could trade," Ocean offered.

Kyle looked over at Ocean to see her biting her lip and trying not to laugh.

"Why were you so distracted, anyway?" she asked, her normal grin returning.

Kyle froze, wondering if he should tell Ocean that Brianna was sitting right next to them. "I was listening to...someone's conversation." He looked down, guilt sweeping through him.

"Okay." Ocean shrugged, though she didn't look convinced. "So, what's your favorite part of this cruise?"

Kyle tried to ignore Brianna and the other girl talking in the background, hoping Ocean wouldn't recognize their voices. "The pool was nice." He winced as Ocean bit her lip. "Though your room is amazing too. And the presentation."

Ocean looked up, smiling. "Yeah, that was pretty cool. Especially when the dolphins swam out of the screen. It was like…" she trailed off, the pained expression filling her face again for a second. She shook her head, and a smirk replaced it. "That was pretty cool that Elizabeth stuck up for you."

Kyle shrugged. "I guess she just wanted to help." Still, he wondered why Elizabeth *had* stuck up for him?

"Kyle, your *omelette* is here." Mrs. Sanders said, teasing.

He looked up just in time to see the waiter put a steaming dish in front of him.

"Enjoy your food." The waiter smiled then hurried to another table.

Kyle and Ocean ate in awkward silence, and he realized that fish and eggs actually went pretty well together.

"So, Ocean…" Paul began as Kyle was taking his last bite of salmon and eggs. "Would you and Kyle like to go and explore the ship together? I know you haven't seen much yet."

Kyle turned toward him, surprised, and he noticed a flicker of hesitation on Paul's face.

"I guess we could go to one of the shops or the garden," Ocean said, sounding a little suspicious.

"Well, then, I guess we're all set," her father said a little too quickly. "Why don't you two go see the aquariums in the garden. I hear they're quite the wonder."

Ocean gave him a nervous look, and he gave her a mischievous grin in return.

"I know what you're thinking, but don't worry, Mrs. Sanders and I aren't dating. We just made friends with each other, like you and Kyle did."

Ocean hesitated, then she and Kyle stood and headed for the wooden walkway leading to the lobby.

"Do you think our parents are just friends?" Ocean asked, looking a little nervous.

Kyle looked down at the pathway, not knowing what to say. Ever since he had come to live with her, Mrs. Sanders had never had any friends, though, he realized, neither had he until he met Ocean.

"I don't think there's too much to worry about." Ocean grinned at him, then spun around and swung the park door open, almost the same way her father did. "My dad has tried to find another wife after my mom died, but he just never can find one who can take her place." For a moment, her eyes darkened, then she looked at him and smiled as a wave of mist hit them.

Kyle tried to ignore the odd feeling in his chest as he walked back into the fields of flowers, and steam wrapped around him. However, the feeling started to ease as the fog engulfed them and he gazed around at the bright flowers in front of the dense rainforest and the blue light shining down from the ceiling. He could almost believe he was in a misty meadow, except that the meadow was waist high, and a cobblestone path led through it.

Kyle started as Ocean slipped past him, and he couldn't help glancing at her prosthetic as she ran her hand across the flowers. He suddenly realized that a few people were staring at Ocean's "leg," and without knowing why, he found himself hanging back. A pang of guilt swept through him as he hurried to catch up with her. The forest grew larger and more majestic the closer they got to it. It was hard to believe they were still in a cruise ship.

"Isn't it amazing?" Ocean asked as they took a fork in the path and headed into the jungle.

Before Kyle could answer, a blue and orange parrot flew in front of him, and he jolted back as it swooped into the canopy above. It nestled into the fronds and cocked its head at him. Suddenly, it let out a squawk.

"What a beautiful forest."

Kyle blinked, not sure he had heard right. It seemed like the parrot was talking.

"How amazing," the parrot screeched, flying onto another branch.

"What was that?" Ocean asked.

Kyle turned to see that she had stopped walking and was looking around at the forest.

"Don't walk off the path," the parrot squawked from above them. "Be careful. I'm watching you."

"Okay, that's one creepy bird," Ocean laughed.

Kyle couldn't break his stare from the parrot, who was still staring at them with its sharp, black eyes, head cocked to one side.

"We should get to the aquarium, though," Ocean said, and Kyle tore his eyes away from the parrot as Ocean started walking again.

They suddenly emerged from the forest, and two huge clouded doors, with long silver handles, appeared from behind the trees.

Ocean grabbed one of the door handles and pulled on it, but the door didn't budge. Kyle scrunched up his forehead, wondering if it was locked. Tentatively, he walked up beside Ocean and grabbed the handle. Together, they pulled, and the door swung inward.

Kyle gazed into the room beyond and a gasp lodged in his throat as he and Ocean stepped inside. Blue and green lights shone down from the ceiling, rippling across the floor toward the two huge aquariums on either side of the room. They stretched along the entire wall and reached up to the ceiling high above. Two giant rocks sat in one, with fish of every color darting around them. High above those, three lemon sharks circled lazily.

Kyle looked over to his left, expecting to see Ocean, but she wasn't there. Looking around, he spotted her by the other aquarium. This one had a tall rock on the side, three rays gliding on its flat surface and blowing the sand off around them.

One of them glided off the rock and came to rest on the sand below, scattering a school of silver fish.

Kyle came up alongside Ocean, staring at the mesmerizing ripples in the water as more rays fluttered off the rock and drifted onto the sand, stirring it around in their wake.

"Oh, look. It's Fish Girl and her sidekick."

Kyle mentally sighed, then spun around to see Brianna standing there with her friend, smirking at him.

"Hey, the fish is frozen," Brianna scoffed, her eyes seeming to light up with fire.

Kyle turned to see Ocean was still staring at the aquarium, though her face was suddenly pale.

"By the way, that was some nice swimming at the pool." Brianna smiled, turning to Kyle, and it almost looked genuine. "You could come swimming with us tonight. You definitely don't need to hang out around girls like Fish Girl here." Brianna's smile suddenly looked fake, and the anger he had felt earlier rushed through him.

"Ocean and I are friends, and friends don't abandon each other." Kyle stared daggers at Brianna, and her smile melted away into anger.

"Well then, Fish Sauce, have fun with *Fish*, and just so you know, Fish Girl doesn't agree with you." Brianna spun around and headed toward a pair of double doors at the end of the room. "I hope you're happy hanging out with a deserter." The bully's friend opened the door and they both walked out into the glittering lobby beyond before letting the door fall shut.

Kyle glanced over at Ocean, who was now staring at the floor biting her lip, and his anger at Brianna suddenly melted away. Taking a deep breath, he walked over to Ocean and put a hand on her shoulder.

"You don't need to be afraid of them now that there are two of us," he said, although he didn't want to meet the bully again anytime soon.

"Thanks," Ocean said quietly, still staring at the floor. Finally she took a deep breath. "Two friends are better than one. That's what my mother used to say to me."

The words Brianna had said suddenly came back to Kyle, and he looked curiously at Ocean. "What did she mean when she said you don't agree with me?"

Ocean's gaze instantly fell to the tiles. "I don't know."

He could tell that she was hiding something, but he decided not to push her.

After a while, Ocean looked back up at the aquarium, and Kyle took his hand off her, watching the fish swim through an A-shaped crack in the rocks.

"You want to know something weird?" she asked suddenly, startling him.

"What?"

"Remember when we crashed into each other? I wasn't paying attention because I was watching someone above us."

"Okay..." What was so special about that?

"I couldn't see the person, but it looked like he or she was staring right at us. Whoever it was looked away as soon as I saw them."

10

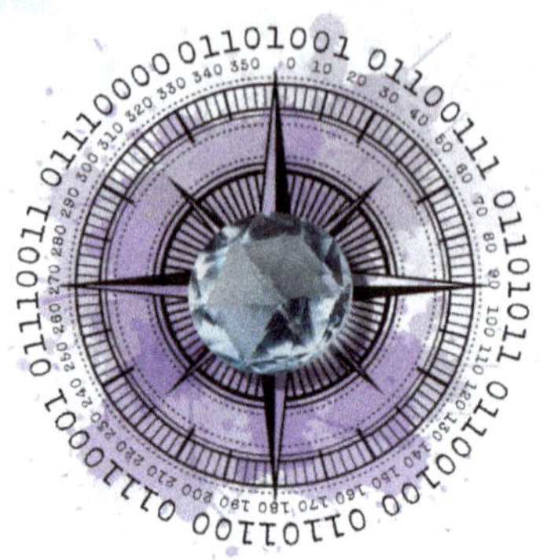

KYLE BOLTED UPRIGHT, HIS heart pounding. Water still seemed to be everywhere and loneliness filled the air. Looking around, all he could see was a shaft of moonlight falling through the window.

Cautiously, he slipped out of his bed, checking to make sure the lump under the covers of Mrs. Sanders' bed hadn't moved. Walking over to the window, he looked out on the moon-lit sea. As soon as he did, he wished he hadn't. The night looked exactly the same as in his dream. Even with Mrs. Sanders there, he still felt the aching loneliness.

He looked back at Mrs. Sanders. Why couldn't she wake up and comfort him like his own mother used to do? He took a deep breath, knowing that his anger was useless. If he wanted Mrs. Sanders awake, all he needed to do was wake her up, but he couldn't.

A glimmer of silver caught his eye from the bedside table. *The necklace.* Kyle silently padded over to it and traced the dolphin with his finger. Taking a deep breath, he took the lid off and held the necklace up to the moonlight. The majestic wooden dolphin dangled from its chain, reflecting silver light.

As he watched it hang there, a sudden ache filled his chest, and he clutched the necklace in his hand as tears slipped down his face. It was his mother's necklace, not his. He shouldn't be the one holding it. Brushing away his tears with one hand, he walked over to the door, putting the necklace around his neck to keep it safe. Checking behind him to make sure Mrs. Sanders hadn't moved, he grabbed the handle, and, before he could decide against it, pulled the door open and stepped out into the hallway.

Apparently, they didn't turn the lights off at night, and Kyle blinked in the sudden brightness, putting his hand in front of his face to shield it. As his eyes got used to the light, he paused, not sure where to go. Something inside him wanted to be out in the night air, but another part of him wanted to stay near Mrs. Sanders. Taking another deep breath, he started down the main corridor, then turned right, heading toward the elevator near the back of the ship.

As he neared the glass elevator, he slowed to a stop, reaching for the button. He hesitated, glancing back down the corridor in the direction of their cabin. He shook his head. Mrs. Sanders wouldn't be waking up for another few hours. There was no way she would know he had left.

He pushed the button, and the elevator door immediately slid open. Cautiously, he stepped inside and pressed the button for the top deck. As soon as the doors closed, he felt the pain return to his chest, and he took a deep breath, wishing the feeling would disappear.

Maybe going off by himself wasn't such a good idea. Looking up, he saw the ceiling approaching quickly, and a few seconds later, he emerged in another identical corridor, and he could see Ocean's room before the elevator rose through the ceiling and surfaced in the room where he had gone with the lifeguard. The chandelier was still glowing, though it looked dimmer and more yellow than before.

The elevator doors slid open, and Kyle walked out onto the plush-carpeted floor. The doors leading outside were right in front of him, but something stopped him from walking over to them. Maybe it was guilt, or maybe he was afraid of going out on deck at night.

Taking a deep breath, he forced himself to walk over and open the doors. For a second, he expected a roaring sea with lightning flashing and waves washing over the deck, but instead, it was completely calm. He slowly let out his breath, taking a step outside, then he gave a muffled gasp. A girl was sitting on the edge of the pool with long hair that reflected the moonlight. It was too dark to make out who it was. He sighed. Why did there always have to be someone everywhere he went? Still, she looked familiar. *Ocean?* Who else would be out by the pool in the middle of the night? Cautiously, he stepped out onto the deck, letting the door swing closed behind him. He started slowly toward the girl, then stopped himself. Even though she was staring at the pool, she could easily turn around and see him. Still, the loneliness he had felt was gone. He wanted someone he could talk to. He closed his eyes, hoping it was Ocean, and continued toward the figure. If it wasn't he could always just say he was lost.

The girl suddenly turned her head toward him, and Kyle froze, his heart pounding. It wasn't Ocean. It was the girl who had been talking with Brianna.

He scanned the deck around him, but he didn't see Brianna herself anywhere. He paused. Would it be weird to just head back for the door and pretend like she wasn't staring at him? Ignoring the heat in his face, he turned around.

"I'm sorry about what happened with you and Ocean at the pool," the girl said, and he turned back to her. *So much for trying to escape.*

The girl looked at him, smiling shyly in the dim light. "I'm Haley, by the way."

"I'm...Kyle," he said, cautiously walking over to her and sitting down on the deck. He pulled at the necklace he had forgotten was there.

"Interesting. Is that short for Kylen?"

He was caught off guard, and Haley's smile brightened.

"No, my full name is just Kyle."

"That's a nice name, but Kylen sounds better," Haley said, then her eyes widened, "And not 'sounds better' like as a name. I mean, I like Kyle, but Kylen just has a nicer ring to it..."

He couldn't help grinning at her. "So, why are you out here in the middle of the night?" he asked, trying to keep out the loneliness starting to creep back in.

"Oh, right," Haley said, scooping up a handful of water and letting it fall back into the pool. "At home, we have a dock behind our house, and every time I just wanted to think, I went out at night and sat on it. I think the waves help me think. And this is the closest thing I have here to the dock." She continued to stare at the water, and she let her smile slip away.

"What were you thinking about?" He didn't want to be nosy, but he couldn't think of anything else to say.

"Pretty much everything that happened today. I thought that when Ocean disappeared, I would never see her again, but now here she is." Haley turned to look at him, and he gave her a puzzled glance.

"I guess you have no idea what I'm talking about," she said, grinning a little. "Ocean used to be on a swim team with us, Brianna and I, and she was great. She basically made up half the team, even though there were six people on it. Well, we were going into a championship, and the prize was huge." Haley splashed her hand in the pool. "Five hundred dollars for every-one on the team. We were pretty sure we would win. Anyway, right before the championship, Ocean quit the team. The coach didn't tell us why, but Brianna was furious. Not surprisingly, we lost."

Haley paused to take a deep breath, staring at the water. "Ocean and Brianna used to be really good friends, and when Ocean came back to school, Brianna tried to get her to join the swim team again, but Ocean refused. After that, Brianna wouldn't have anything to do with her." Haley let her hand dip into the water, and she closed her eyes. "Then, Brianna started teasing Ocean about her fear. I tried to get her to stop, but she wouldn't. Ocean started to steer clear of Brianna, and then she disappeared."

"So, Ocean didn't stop swimming because of her...leg?" He inwardly winced.

"Oh, that?" Haley asked, surprised, "I think she's always had a prosthetic. I guess it was kind of weird at first. We all teased her and thought she was going to be the slowest, but she proved us all wrong. I guess we grew used to it, though. Back then, she only had a waterproof one, but I guess she got rid of it, or maybe she grew out of it."

Kyle looked out across the water at the platform sticking out on the other side, remembering what had happened just that morning. "So, why are you still friends with Brianna?" He immediately regretted asking that. *Why can't I just mind my own business?*

"Because, we agreed to be best friends forever," Haley said, like it was the simplest thing in the world. "Plus, if I left her, she wouldn't have any friends at all."

Kyle looked down at the wooden deck. He certainly couldn't see how Brianna deserved to have any friends.

"Of course, losing a friend over five hundred dollars is still wrong." Haley stared down at the water. "Friends are supposed to stay together even when they change. She's wrong, you know. Ocean didn't desert her. Brianna's the one who didn't want anything to do with Ocean." Haley looked across the water. "So, why are *you* here in the middle of the night?"

He blinked. Of course he should have expected that. "I was just...taking a walk." His face heated up, and he turned away from her. She had been completely honest with him, and now he was lying to her.

"Then I guess I was too," Haley said hotly, and he dropped his eyes.

He took a deep breath. "I had a nightmare." As soon as he said it, he wished he hadn't.

"Oh," Haley said quietly. "about what?"

Kyle tried to force the memory out of his mind, but he couldn't. The ocean surrounding him, pulling him under. The flooded cabin. His father screaming at him to run. Feeling the tears starting to come, he looked back down at the water.

"You don't have to tell me," Haley said, putting a hand on his arm. He instinctively flinched.

"I'll try to keep Brianna away from you guys." She smiled, and Kyle felt a new kind of pain hit him, like the pain when his father would put rubbing alcohol on a cut on his leg. It was completely different from the one he had felt in the nightmare, and it felt almost nice.

"Thanks," he whispered, staring out at the pitch black ocean. "Sometimes I wonder if they're still out there." He glanced at Haley to see how she would respond, but she was just staring at the pool. After an awkward silence, she looked up, her eyes glossy.

"Sometimes I wonder if my dad will ever write to me. He left when I was a baby, right after my mom died. Left me with my aunt and just took off. I don't even know where he is." She looked away, and when she looked back at him, she was smiling again. "Anyway, I'd better go back to my room before Brianna wakes up and comes looking for me." She paused, narrowing her eyes. "And I bet your mom wouldn't be very happy if she found you gone either."

He felt a fresh wave of guilt, and Haley's smile grew again.

"And maybe at least *try* to stay with her from now on. Really, you might get yourself into trouble." She winked, then started for the cabins. Kyle watched her disappear through the doors, feeling the cold breeze blow against him. Maybe she wasn't that bad. And maybe, just maybe, they wouldn't have to deal with Brianna anymore. Although he doubted it. He had a feeling she wouldn't stop until she got what she wanted: getting back at Ocean. But he wasn't about to let her do that.

11

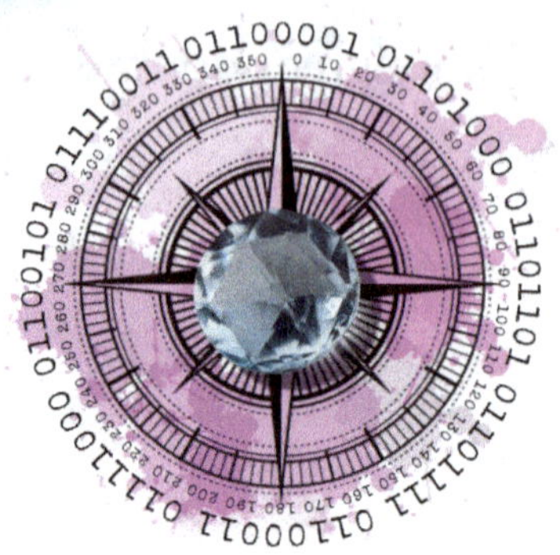

"KYLE, TIME TO WAKE up," Mrs. Sanders said, shaking him gently. "Our breakfast is here. I figured we would eat in our cabin."

Kyle looked up at her, blinking away the blurriness in the bright light. The scent of fresh pancakes filled the room, and with it the memories of the night before. For a moment, he wondered if it had all been a dream. *No, it had been too vivid for a dream.*

He looked over to where a wooden tray was sitting with two steaming stacks of pancakes. Throwing off the covers, he leaped onto the carpet, feeling something light and hard bounce against his neck. Curiously, he fingered the wooden figurine and his heart seemed to freeze. He was still wearing the dolphin necklace from last night.

He glanced at Mrs. Sanders, hoping that she hadn't noticed. If she had, didn't show it as she just gestured to the platter of food.

"Our breakfast, monsieur," Mrs. Sanders said in a perfect French accent.

Kyle tried to ignore the burning in his face as he walked over to her bed, clutching his necklace in his hand. Taking his plate, he ladled some syrup that smelled like peaches onto one of his pancakes.

As he and Mrs. Sanders started eating, his thoughts returned to the night before. Maybe he would meet Haley again, and if she kept her promise, *never* meet Brianna again. How Haley would stop her, though, he had no idea.

Kyle looked down at his plate to get another bite, then stopped, confused. On his plate was a fresh pancake topped with chocolate chips and slices of strawberry. Had he been so caught up in his thoughts that he made a new pancake? Or...he glanced at Mrs. Sanders to see her trying hard not to laugh.

"Sorry. I couldn't help myself," she said, switching their plates back. "You just were just staring off into space."

He finished off four more pancakes before heading to the bathroom to get dressed.

As he came out he found Mrs. Sanders trying to pull open the top drawer of her bedside table. He grinned as she tugged and finally yanked it out enough to push the clothes down so it would slide out all the way.

"Guess I filled it a bit too much," she said, smiling awkwardly as she turned to look at him. He noticed the lower drawer was also bulging, but he decided not to point that out.

Mrs. Sanders sighed as she turned back to the bedside table and started taking clothes out, then paused again to look back at him. He stood there awkwardly, and his hand went back to the necklace. Finally, he couldn't stand the silence.

"Can I go over to Ocean's room?" he asked, and Mrs. Sanders looked up, blinking in surprise.

"Sure. I'll probably be about half an hour anyway." A smirk replaced her surprise. "Just make sure to come back in half an hour." She gave him a pointed look, then turned back to her clothes.

He stood there, his stomach suddenly tied up in knots. Had he just asked to go to Ocean's room? The girl he had just met yesterday? What if she was still sleeping? What if she didn't even want him to come over? There was only one way to find out. Fighting his thoughts, he turned and headed out of the cabin. The warm lights on the sides of the hallway seemed to be brighter than last time he had been here. Hurrying down the corridor, he turned left, headed for the elevator. Suddenly, he heard footsteps behind him, and before he could turn around, someone grabbed his arm, hard.

"Look, I'm going to make one thing clear, *Fish Sauce*." Brianna's voice came from right next to his ear. "You either stay out of my way or you'll regret it."

Kyle swallowed as heat rushed through him. He spun around, glaring at the girl who had apparently been following him. "I'm not going to let you hurt Ocean! We're friends, and friends don't abandon each other."

For a moment, he saw a flicker of hurt in Brianna's face. Then, she glared back at him. "I'm sure Haley talked to you last night, but she doesn't know even half of the story. I'm not going to let you get in the way, Kyle."

Kyle blinked. She had actually used his name for once. *For that matter, how does she even know my name?*

"Okay, how about this," he said, trying not to sound as scared as he felt. Brianna just cocked her head at him, smirking. "We'll have a showdown. If I win, you won't go near Ocean for the rest of the trip."

"And if I win" —Brianna scrunched up her nose at him— "you have to stay out of my way and let me give Ocean what she deserves. Oh, and if you don't show up, I automatically win."

Kyle swallowed. *Turn around. Back out. This is a crazy idea!* His brain screamed at him. He gritted his teeth. "Fine."

"Great! Then meet me at the Sapphire Pool at 12 o'clock." With that, she spun and headed back the way she had come, strutting like she'd already won, which she probably had.

As he stared after her, his anger faded, and in the sudden quiet, his stomach churned. How in the world was he supposed to beat her in the water? What had he just agreed to?

KYLE RAISED HIS HAND to knock, then stopped. Maybe it was a little early to be at Ocean's door. Taking a deep breath, he gave a tentative knock. He waited a few seconds. *Nothing.* Maybe Ocean was eating breakfast somewhere, or sleeping. As he turned around and headed away, he heard a door opening, and light flooded the hallway.

"Kyle?" Paul asked from behind him. Kyle spun around as Ocean joined her father in the doorway leading to their under-water-themed room.

"Oh, hi," Ocean said, walking out into the hallway to meet him. "What are you doing here?"

Kyle looked down, not sure what to say. "I was wondering if you wanted to go exploring."

"Actually," Paul said with a twinkle in his eye, "we were just about to go find *you*."

"There's a presentation in the kids' area," Ocean said, grinning. "It's supposed to be like you're actually in the movie."

Kyle hesitated. "I'll have to ask Mrs. Sanders first. I have to be back soon."

For a moment, Ocean looked confused, then she shook her head, grinning again. "We can just ask her. I'm sure she would be fine with it. Come on." She headed out the door, and Kyle glanced at her father, who gave him a thumbs-up.

"Just come back after you're done," Paul called after them as they walked down the hallway.

Ocean gave him a thumbs-up of her own, then turned to Kyle. "How long have you lived with...Mrs. Sanders?"

Kyle looked down at the carpet, suddenly realizing why she had looked confused. Had he really called her Mrs. Sanders? He swallowed, feeling his chest tighten.

"About two years." As soon as he said it, a vision of him meeting Mrs. Sanders flashed in his mind, and he shook his head, focusing on the little diamond patterns in the carpet. Still, he couldn't shake the pain or the feeling of loss that he'd felt when he'd met her.

"My mom disappeared a year ago," Ocean suddenly said, breaking the silence.

Kyle looked up, blinking.

"She left and...never came back," she continued. Shaking her head, she started walking again. "Come on. The presentation is going to start soon."

Shaking himself, he followed Ocean into the elevator, and they began their descent.

KYLE IMMEDIATELY FELT THE change as he and Ocean neared the huge tree trunk doorway with "Welcome to the Tree House" written with sticks above it. Of course Mrs. Sanders had said yes, although she probably would have agreed to be fed to the sharks, since she had been studying a piece of paper and only half paying attention. Either way, they were here!

As the two of them walked through the doorway, he felt like he had walked into a jungle. The whole room was a dark green, with vines running along the walls and ceiling, and a canopy of leaves draped down toward him. The only thing that didn't quite fit was the large glass window that looked out onto the ocean and an open glass tank, stingrays gliding on the sandy bottom.

"Wow..." Ocean whispered, slowing as she gazed around the room, and Kyle had to admit it was amazing, although it didn't compare to the rainforest downstairs.

"We should come here sometime just to hang out." She grinned, looking over to where the stingray tank rested.

Just as she was about to say something else, lively music started playing from every direction, and Beth's voice filled the air.

"Alrighty! Who's ready for an adventure?"

From a room on their right came the sound of kids cheering.

"Those of you in the main room, please head toward the big metal door."

"Come on. It's about to start," Ocean said excitedly, already heading toward a door with a wheel on it, like from an old ship. He hurried after her, jogging past the treehouse, and together they entered the room.

All he could see was a curved narrow dark-gray space with two rows of seats crowded with kids. The young woman from the presentation stood in front of a large blank panel at the end of the room.

"All right, everyone," she said, silencing the group, "take a seat." Her sharp eyes scanned the room.

"As you all probably know by now," she began, "my name's Elizabeth Quigley. However, here you can call me Beth." She faced them with a cunning grin. "Prepare yourselves. You're about to observe something not many people get to see. What if I told you that this room was actually a submarine, and could take us into the depths of the ocean?"

Kyle looked around, seeing that some faces seemed to be astonished, while others looked skeptical. Glancing at Ocean sitting next to him, he could see she was smirking, though she hesitated a bit.

"Okay, I'll let you in on a secret. This presentation is a simulation. We will not actually be leaving the ship, but pretend for a second that we can."

With that, the door behind them slowly swung shut, and the lights dimmed.

"Captain, begin our descent!" she commanded, and there was a jolt that raised gasps around the room.

"While we descend, I'll tell you a little of what you're about to see. Right now, we're sailing out into the Gulf of Mexico, off the Florida Keys, a place swarming with bottlenose dolphins, hammerhead sharks, and other warm-water aquatic animals." She walked to the middle of the wall in front of them and pressed her hand into it. Slowly, it rose, and Kyle, along with almost everyone in the room, gasped. Through the now revealed glass, he could see gray streaks whipping by as they descended.

"We are now entering the sunlight zone." Beth gestured out the window as the "submarine" slowed down and they emerged into the ocean. Above them, Kyle could see the ship with two huge propellers in the middle slowly spinning around.

Everyone was silent as they stared out of the window at the ocean stretching before them, eventually disappearing into a blue fog.

"And this," Beth said, "is what it looks like under a cruise ship."

Looking at the ship from the outside while being *inside* it was weird, kind of like watching himself.

"Now, we just put on a little music and wait for the animals to arrive."

Faintly, mysterious music echoed around them. It almost sounded like underwater music for a documentary, and Kyle wondered if it was meant more for them than the animals.

"It almost feels real," he breathed. When Ocean didn't respond, he turned to see her eyes were closed, and she was breathing heavily.

His mind raced, wondering if she was going to pass out again as Beth turned around and pressed one of the buttons that had flickered on, and the submarine lurched again.

"Now, forward and onward!" she asserted as the room seemed to shoot through the water and away from the ship. Suddenly, a patch of sand emerged from the dark-blue fog, and as they got closer, he could see that it was the ocean floor. He glanced back at Ocean, who still looked like she was about to faint.

Taking a deep breath, he started to stand up, but without warning, the room shuddered and he fell back into his seat. The room seemed to slow down until it was gliding over the sand. In front of them, a brightly colored coral reef appeared from the blueness, and he caught sight of a small shark swimming around it.

"Now, you've probably seen our lemon sharks in the aquariums by this point."

At this remark from Beth, Ocean opened her eyes, and for a moment she seemed to forget her fear.

"However, this is a much larger breed of shark."

The submarine slowly approached the coral reef as another small form emerged from the fog, then three. As the submarine neared the sharks, Kyle saw that they were bigger than he had first thought, and even though he knew he wasn't really there, a pang of fear swept through him.

"These are Caribbean reef sharks," Beth said as one of the sharks brushed past the window. "Right now, it looks as if they're feeding. The Caribbean reef shark has a cunning tactic for catching its prey. First, it will lazily swim in the general direction of the fish it's after, like one of them is doing now."

Kyle looked out the window. *All* the sharks were swimming around. How could he tell which was aiming, or not aiming, for a fish?

"It's the one on the far left," Ocean whispered, and he glanced at her, surprised to see that she no longer looked as afraid.

"Once it is close enough, the reef shark will dart past the fish, as if after another fish, then, without warning, whip around and snatch the fish in its jaws." As Beth spoke, one of the sharks darted forward, and just like she'd said, it spun around, grabbing a fish it had swum past. "Now, there's so much more I could say about this amazing creature, but let's move onward." With that, the room lurched forward again, and Ocean scrunched her eyes closed.

"Down here in this coral reef, we're bound to see other animals, such as turtles, fish, and rays." As Beth said this, the room zipped past a ray gliding on the ocean floor. "But what we're looking for now is a certain cetacean you are all pretty familiar with."

A loud, piercing whistle echoed around the room, and Kyle caught his breath. He recognized that sound. It was the sound he had heard every time he went out with his mother on her trips. The sound he always strained his ears to hear, even sometimes in his bedroom at night. *Dolphins.*

"Right now, I'm sending out a signature whistle from the submarine. Dolphins use these whistles to call to each other, but not in the way we do. While we would normally call someone else's name, dolphins call their own names to let other dolphins know they're there." Beth looked like she was about to speak, when another whistle pierced through the air. "And it looks like someone found us."

As if on cue, the sleek form of a bottlenose dolphin appeared out of the blue mist and darted toward them. Kyle caught his breath as the majestic animal slowed down and peered through the window at them, letting out a stream of bubbles from its blowhole.

"Right now, the dolphin is emitting high frequency clicks of 120 kilohertz to try to figure out what we are. Since most humans can hear only as high as 18 kilohertz, it is far above our hearing range, and so we can't hear a thing. However, if we bring it into a range we *can* hear, it sounds like this." A rapid clicking filled the room. Even though he knew this was a simulation, he was drawn to the window, and everything in him wanted to touch the dolphin.

Then, with a quick stroke of its tail, the dolphin swam up and out of view of the window.

"Now, I'm afraid our time is up, so, captain, begin our ascent!"

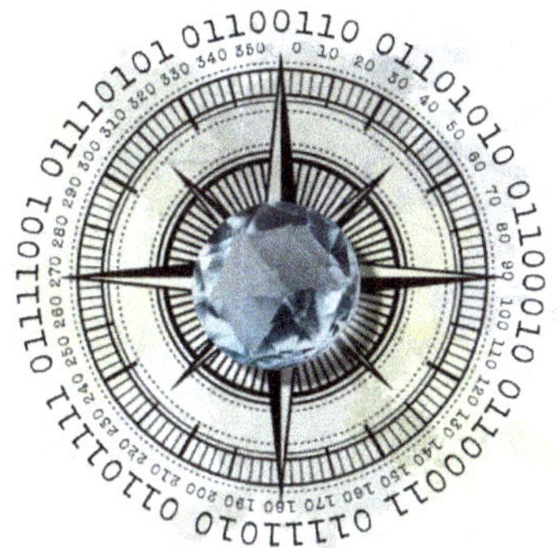

"That was amazing," Ocean said as they got up from their seats and headed for the exit. Kyle couldn't help but smile. Maybe it hadn't actually been real, but Ocean was right. It had definitely been amazing.

Someone tapped him on the shoulder, and he spun around to see Beth standing there, smiling.

"Can I steal a few minutes with you?" she asked, her cheery smile fading a bit.

Kyle glanced at Ocean, who shrugged, just as confused as he was.

"Uhh...sure," he replied. What could she want with him?

As soon as the last child had left, Beth turned back to him and Ocean.

"I just wanted to say that what you did yesterday at the pool was an extremely brave thing to do. No matter what anyone says, don't ever give up that courage."

Kyle's face started to heat up, and he looked down as a warmth spread through him. It was the same feeling he had gotten, back when he was little, when his mother had said that he had cleaned his room by himself, or when his father had said his attempt at a carved dolphin looked beautiful. The warmth inside seemed to disappear as he thought about his parents, and he shook his head.

"I'll be around if you want to talk with me…" She paused, and Kyle realized he'd never told her his name.

"Kyle," he said, looking up at her again. She looked a lot younger than he had first thought, maybe only about twenty or thirty.

"Kyle, you're braver than anyone I know." Beth said, a hint of admiration in her voice. "If you ever need anything, you can usually find me in the café on the top deck. Unfortunately, I have business to get to. See you around." She winked before heading out of the room. Suddenly, he remembered Ocean. He turned to her, swallowing when he saw she was looking away, her face red.

"Uh, Ocean?" He hesitated, then walked over to her and awkwardly placed his hand on her shoulder. Her head snapped up and he jerked his hand away.

"You're brave because I can't fight for myself!" Ocean snapped.

He stared at her, bewildered. "That's not—"

"You don't know what it's like! You don't know what happened!" Ocean's eyes filled with tears, and she abruptly turned away again.

"But I—" He felt his heart pounding as he tried to get the words out. "I do know."

"No you don't! Everyone says they do, but they can't. I didn't until—" Ocean broke off, biting her lip.

He looked at her, realizing that they weren't talking about the bully anymore. He bit back a rebuttal, knowing that wouldn't help. "Ocean, I lost my parents too. They're both..." His breath caught in his throat, and a sharp pain stabbed in his chest. *They're both dead.* Even thinking it, he felt the room starting to sway.

"I'm sorry." Ocean's suddenly quiet voice startled Kyle. "I just wanted to be different. I don't want to be afraid of the water. I'm sorry I brought up my mom."

Kyle felt a hand on his shoulder, and he forced himself not to pull away. After a few seconds, the room stopped spinning, and all he was left with was a cold, aching pain in his chest.

"Maybe we should go to my cabin and talk," Ocean suggested, her anger gone.

"I don't want to talk about it," Kyle said, trying to force the pain down.

"Well, then, at least I can tell you what happened to my mom. Come on."

He didn't respond, but he followed his friend out into the green-carpeted area.

As the two of them headed down the hallway to Ocean's cabin, he couldn't stop the memories that swirled around him. A memory of a rainy day flashed through his mind. His mother had been planning a beach day for a week and she wasn't about to let some rain get in the way. So while it was pouring, they had set off, dressed in their bathing suits. When they got there, already soaked, they'd found the usually crowded beach completely empty. He smiled at the memory, remembering how they'd tried to save their sand castle from the "acid rain", until the rain got so bad they had to go home.

His thoughts were cut off by the click of the lock on Ocean's door. He paused at the doorway as she headed over to the far bed and hopped up onto it, patting the blanket beside her. He hesitated a moment before hopping up next to her. She grinned, then bit her lip.

"I guess I said I would tell you about my mom." She sounded uneasy all of a sudden. Taking a deep breath, she started, "When I was about ten, my dad bought a fishing boat for my mom, since she loved the water, but he never took her sailing. He was always busy with work, even on the weekends, and he never really had time for either of us. We only got to talk to each other right before I went to bed." Ocean paused, a faraway look in her eyes. After a second, she shook her head and continued.

"I don't think my mom was ever mad at him for it. She stayed home and taught me, so we needed someone to work to support us. Then, one day, my mom got tired of waiting for my dad to go sailing with her. So she just got in the boat and took off. She said she had read enough to know what to do. The last thing I saw of her was her smiling and waving to me as she sailed off into the ocean." Ocean bit her lip, looking away.

"Then, a tropical storm hit our home. My dad came back early to make sure everything was all tucked away and safe, and I told him that Mom had gone sailing that morning and hadn't returned." Ocean paused again for a moment and sniffed. Kyle looked down at the carpet, a vision flashing though his mind of his own mother falling into the ocean.

"He immediately called the Coast Guard, and they sent out a rescue party. A day later, Dad said they had found the remains of the boat. They never found my mom, and they concluded that she had crashed into a rocky outcrop and...died." Tears suddenly ran down Ocean's face, and she looked down at the carpet.

Kyle didn't realize he had put his hand on her shoulder until he felt her shaking, and he instinctively pulled his hand away. Ocean let out a choked laugh, and she looked up at him, wiping her tears on her sleeve.

Something in him wanted to tell her everything about his own parents, but he couldn't. "So, where's your dad?" he asked instead, trying to break the silence in the room.

Ocean looked up again, curious. "Oh, I guess he's—" She paused suddenly, her eyes drifting to the bed. "I guess he's probably with your..." She looked at him sheepishly. "Uh, what do you call her?"

He forced himself not to look away. "I just call her Mrs. Sanders." It sounded weird actually saying it out loud. "But you can call her my mom."

"I guess he's with your 'my mom', then," Ocean said, smirking at him.

A knock came from the door, and he jumped. Silently, Ocean slipped off the bed and padded over to the door, peering through the peephole.

"It's…your mom," Ocean said, opening the door to reveal Mrs. Sanders standing in the dim light of the hallway.

As Mrs. Sanders stepped into the room, Kyle instantly saw the wrinkles on her forehead, and his heart froze. The only time he had ever seen her like that was when he had fallen down the stairs and hit his head, but this time she looked different.

"Kyle, come with me," she said, her voice shaking. "Someone broke into our room."

M RS. SANDERS PRESSED HER hands into her forehead as she stared at the note on the table. Finally, she looked up, frowning.

"It doesn't make any sense. Why would someone just leave a note in our room?!" She looked like she was about to say something, then stopped herself, and the only sound that filled the silence was the soft lapping from the pool and an excited toddler screeching from the pool area. Kyle looked up at the open umbrella above them, not sure what to do. Mrs. Sanders still wouldn't tell him what the note said, and anytime he tried to peek at it, she would put it back in her purse, only to take it out a minute later and read it again. He looked back down to see Mrs. Sanders studying it intently.

"Signed, a friend," she muttered, and Kyle glanced up expectantly, though she didn't read any more.

"Can I help you with anything?" a man asked from behind them, and Mrs. Sanders quickly looked up, sticking the note back in her purse.

For the twentieth time, he thought, fighting the urge to just take the note from her.

"Oh. No, we're fine," she said, looking up at him.

"All right, just making sure." He gave them a long glance, then headed away.

Mrs. Sanders let out a big sigh, then stood up, scooting her chair out from the table. "Okay. We're calling security," she said, starting to walk away. Kyle sprang to his feet, hurrying to catch up with her. A gust of wind blew around him, and something fluttered out of her purse, landing silently on the deck. He scooped it up before it could blow away, and almost handed it to her, then froze. It was the note.

Heart pounding, he flipped it over, expecting the page to be covered in words. Instead, there was only one line, and he almost dropped the note as he read it.

Fiona Sanders, your cover is compromised. Get your-
self and Kyle off the ship as soon as possible. Beware
the thorn. —a friend

He stared at the note, letting it flutter in the wind. Mrs. Sanders quickly snatched it away. "I didn't want you to see that," she said, a little too harshly.

"What does it mean?" he asked. It felt like he had eaten a handful of rocks. Maybe it was all some sort of prank and his adoptive mom would break out in a grin.

"It means exactly what it sounds like." There was a quiver in her voice that he had never heard before. "They found us."

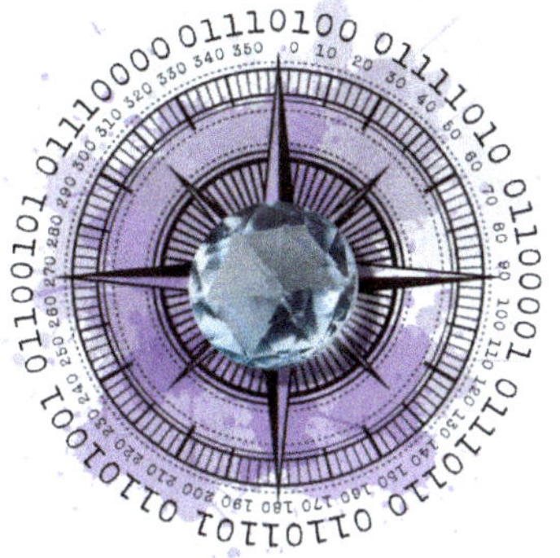

KYLE PUSHED THE GRILLED cheese sandwich around his plate as he tried to piece everything together. *They found us?* Who had found them? Since they had gotten lunch, Mrs. Sanders hadn't said anything other than muttering to herself. If someone had found them, then the person had to be on the cruise with them. The thought sent a shiver up his spine. It could be anyone on the ship.

"Kyle, are you going to eat that?" Mrs. Sanders asked, her voice filled with concern.

He looked down at his sandwich, biting his lip. There was no use in trying to force it down.

"You must be pretty hungry if you're going to eat your lip," Mrs. Sanders said, letting out a forced chuckle, and he looked up at her, scowling. "Look, Kyle. I didn't mean what I said. We don't know if the note is even true. It could just be an elaborate joke."

Her tone was reassuring, but it was only a coverup. She knew it was real. Why else would she have said, "They found us"?

"Kyle, you can't go the whole trip without eating."

Reluctantly, Kyle took a bite, surprised that the sandwich still tasted good. Maybe Mrs. Sanders was right. Somehow he had expected it to taste like cardboard, like in all the books he'd read. Maybe the note was nothing, even though he could see that his adoptive mom didn't really believe that either.

Suddenly uneasy, he turned around. Was someone watching him, or was it just his imagination? The only people he could see were the ones in line for Bravo's Bistro and two grandparents playing with a toddler in the pool. They wouldn't be watching him, would they? As he scanned the deck again, all he wanted to do was find Ocean, and figure out who had broken in, and why.

"Well," Mrs. Sanders sighed, "If you're not going to eat that sandwich, we can head over to the top deck. I'm meeting Paul there, and I'm sure Ocean will be with him."

Kyle wrinkled his forehead, wondering for a split second if Mrs. Sanders actually *could* read his mind. He quickly got up, grabbing the sandwich off the table. She gave him a surprised look, then turned around and headed for one of the winding staircases.

THE LAPPING OF WATER mixed with the screeching of children filled the air as Kyle gazed down at the light wooden deck.

"Maybe someone did it just to make you think you're being followed so that it ruins the rest of your cruise," Ocean suggested.

"But who would do that?" he asked, even though he knew she was just trying to lighten the mood. Other than Brianna, he couldn't think of anyone who wanted to ruin his cruise, and how could she break into their room without them noticing? Ocean's only response was to bite her lip and look down at the deck.

"Well, either way, you can't let a threat ruin the cruise. Someone must have just..." She trailed off, frowning.

"What?" he demanded, his fear returning. "Why would some do this?!"

"I just don't understand how someone could have gotten into your room. They must have somehow unlocked the door and disabled the security cameras, unless it was the cleaning lady." She grinned. "In the stories it's always the cleaning lady or the butler who does it."

"You're not helping," Kyle groaned, imagining a cleaning lady rummaging through their room.

"Sorry. But, Kyle, no matter what happens, I'll help you through it. If you can get past Brianna, we can definitely get past this." She gave him a small smile, then gazed across the pool. "If whoever wrote the note is telling the truth, what do you think they want?"

"I don't know. Maybe my mom made enemies of some kind..." It sounded too weird to be true, though. Mrs. Sanders wasn't some kind of secret agent. She was just a goofy, slightly scatterbrained woman who loved pancakes.

"So, what do we do now?" Ocean asked. Her icy eyes seemed to bore into him.

"Maybe security will figure out who wrote the note," he suggested instead. "I guess all we do is wait."

"But then what if the note is true? They still won't know who the note was warning you about," she said, apparently too wrapped up in the mystery to stop.

"Yeah, I guess so. It still—" Kyle's words were cut off by a sickeningly familiar voice behind them.

"Oh, hey there, *Detective Fish Sauce*," the voice said, and his heart skipped a beat.

Spinning around, he glared at Brianna.

"Or maybe I should call you *chicken*." She matched his scowl with a much fiercer one.

Chicken?

"Or did you just *forget* about your promise?"

His heart sank, her words coming back to him. "*Meet me at the Sapphire Pool at 12 o'clock.*" That had been hours ago. *When Mrs. Sanders found the note.* "I didn't say I would go." He tried to sound confident, but it came out more as a murmur.

"Oh, really? Because I'm sure you said 'fine, we'll have a show-down.' But of course you were only saying that. Still, the rule applies. You agreed to stay out of my way."

Kyle started to protest, and a disgusted look came over Brianna's face.

"Oh, right. Friends don't abandon each other."

Please just go away! he thought, but he didn't dare say it. He knew what was coming next even before she said it.

"Why don't you tell your friend that? In fact, why don't you tell her that you know everything. Why don't you tell her how you were talking with Haley in the middle of the night. Now I get why you two became friends. You're both cowards." Just like that, she spun around and stalked away, leaving him to face Ocean. *Probably on purpose.*

After a moment, Ocean took a deep breath. "Don't worry about her. She's always like that."

He couldn't respond, or even meet her eyes. Silence followed, and he was sure that she would see straight through him.

"Kyle?"

Finally, he looked up, guilt burning through him. "Brianna and I bumped into each other in the hallway, and she challenged me to a—"

Ocean cut off his words. "So it's true? You *have* been talking to Haley? You don't understand what happened!" she yelled, getting to her feet. "You couldn't know what they did to me!"

"But Haley isn't..." He trailed off. She wasn't listening to him. He wished he could take his words back, but it was too late. Why had he ever challenged Brianna?!

"Haley was there!" she exclaimed. "She didn't care—" Tears trickled down her face. "No one cared." She paused for a second, taking a shaky breath. "I thought you cared." Then she got up and walked past him.

It felt like a knife had been thrust into his heart, and he looked down, guilt washing over him. He wanted to say he was sorry, but he couldn't make any words come out. She would never forgive him now anyway.

Kyle felt the loneliness settle over him like the humid air.

Before meeting Ocean, he had gotten used to the loneliness. Now, it hit him full force, and he stared out at the water, wondering if it would ever leave again. All he knew was that he suddenly didn't have a friend, and it was all Brianna's fault. She was going to pay.

"CLINT, COULD YOU RUN this to the lab and check for fingerprints?" The burly officer handed Mrs. Sanders' note to another officer, who took it and headed through a glass door. "Now, tell me again how you found that note," the first officer said, turning back to her and taking out a pad and pen.

Mrs. Sanders took a deep breath, then repeated her story. "I told Kyle to go explore the ship while I organized the cabin. After I was done, I went into the bathroom. I thought I heard the lock click, but that could have just been my imagination. I didn't notice anything odd when I left the bathroom, and I was about to leave when I saw that Kyle's drawer was hanging open, and—" She stopped abruptly, biting her lip, and the officer glanced up from his scribbling to nod at her. She took a deep breath, then continued, "I was just about to close it when I remembered that Kyle hadn't opened it, and I was sure it was closed when he left. Immediately, I checked to make sure his mother's necklace was still there, and when I saw it was, I almost closed the drawer, until I saw the slip of paper poking out from under the box…" She trailed off, shaking her head and taking a deep breath. "You know the rest."

"Yes ma'am. You did the right thing by coming to us. We assure you that if this note was from one of our crew, they will be punished severely. This is not a matter to be taken lightly." The man shook Mrs. Sanders' hand, then turned his gaze to Kyle.

"Is there anything you would like to add?" The officer looked at him pointedly, and Kyle tensed, wondering if he should tell the officer about the clerk with the identical necklace. Finally, he shook his head, and the officer smiled.

"All right then, have a nice cruise, and don't worry about that note. We'll take it from here. Just remember to always stay with at least one other person at all times. Come back if you get any more notes or if you notice anything out of the ordinary, such as someone following you."

"Right…" Mrs. Sanders sighed, then turned around and headed out of the office. Kyle hurried after her, glancing back to see the guard smile after them before disappearing through the glass door.

"Well, *that* was helpful," Mrs. Sanders said, shaking her head as she led Kyle through the bright white hallway toward the elevator they had taken down to the office. "There are 57 crew members, and it could be any of them."

He was about to ask her how she knew the number of crew members, when the clerk at the jewelry shop flashed through his mind again, and he bit his lip, wondering if he should tell Mrs. Sanders about the man. It couldn't hurt for her to know, since she already knew about his dolphin necklace. It was now or never.

He took a deep breath. "There is one—" His words were suddenly cut off as the lights above them flickered, and they were plunged into darkness. He heard Mrs. Sanders' footsteps stop, and he could feel her tense.

"All right, Kyle, don't move. We'll just wait until the lights come back—"

The lights blinked back on and the captain's voice crackled through the speakers.

"Attention, all passengers. That small blackout you just experienced was due to a malfunction in the generator. The power has been switched to our backup batteries while we fix the problem. Some conveniences have been shut down to save energy, such as elevators, pool filters, and pretty much anything that isn't used for lighting or navigational purposes." The speakers crackled a bit then continued. "If you are presently trapped inside an elevator, please press the help button, and a crew member will manually supply power to your elevator. Thank you for being patient as we work on restoring the power." At that, the speakers gave a final crackle and the hallway was filled with silence.

"Well, I guess we're stuck here, then," Mrs. Sanders said, turning to Kyle with a worried smile. "Perhaps we should head back to the guard office."

Kyle nodded as he followed her back the way they had just come. As they neared the doors, a chill suddenly ran through him. What if the person the note had been warning about had cut the power? *What if it's one of the guards?*

"Maybe we should..." he started to say, but Mrs. Sanders cut him off, a look of resolve on her face.

"Kyle, I think it's time I told you the truth."

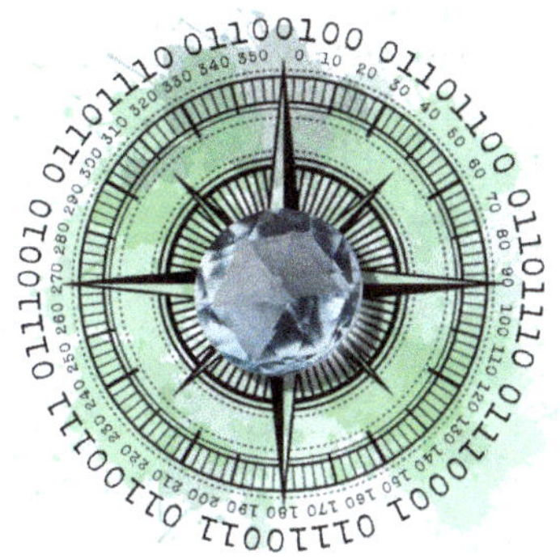

14

"Let's head over to the garden where it's more quiet." Mrs. Sanders almost had to shout over the noise of the crowd that had gathered in the lobby. Luckily a guard had activated the elevator for them and escorted them here. Unfortunately, every other passenger also seemed to be here, crowding the entire lobby so he could barely see ten feet in front of him. Following closely behind Mrs. Sanders, he headed for the stairs. Suddenly, he was cut off by a group passing between them and his heart started to race. Fighting his way through, he found himself walking deeper into the cluster of people. Just like that, Mrs. Sanders was gone.

Taking a deep breath, he paused, trying not to panic. Everywhere around him, people shifted and crowded his view. He could just make out a balcony through the heads, and he headed in that direction, hoping it was the way to the gardens.

The noise of concerned and annoyed voices clouded his thoughts and he tried to block them out. Suddenly, a voice he recognized drifted by, and he turned to see Ocean holding her father's hand. There was a look of confusion on her face as she  seemed to be scanning the crowd. A jab went through him while he watched her. Why couldn't he just apologize to her? But apologize for what? All he had done was talk to Haley. He froze as Ocean glanced his way. She started, the same hurt, angry look returning to her face. She looked away, obviously ignoring him.

Kyle felt anger rise up in him as he turned away and headed for the balcony. It wasn't fair that Ocean was mad at him because of what Brianna did to her. He had nothing to do with it. He pushed through the people, nearing the edge of the lobby.

"Kyle! There you are!" Mrs. Sanders shouted from somewhere nearby. Kyle scanned the room, catching sight of her as she waved to him. Relaxing, he made his way to her.

"They've closed down the gardens since there's no lights on inside." She gave him a quick hug, and he tensed. "So it looks like we'll have to hang out in the shops." With that, she turned and headed under the cover of the balcony. Soft yellow lights illuminated the passageway, with dark shop windows on either side.

"Well. Looks like everything's closed right now."

Kyle nodded, preparing to turn around, but Mrs. Sanders continued on toward the double doors at the end of the line of shops. Before he could ask where they were going, his adoptive mom reached out and pulled one open. A long, low whistle came from inside, followed by clicks and groans with underwater noises in the background. Spellbound, he stepped into the dim room, and the sounds were suddenly all around them.

"Turns out they didn't turn everything off," Mrs. Sanders whispered as Kyle gazed around at the huge aquariums spanning both of the walls. "They must have just set it to night mode."

"Attention, ladies and gentlemen!" The captain's voice shattered the eeriness of the room. "We have fixed the problem. I am now restoring power to the ship. All of our facilities will soon be operating normally. Thank you for your patience and have a wonderful evening!" As soon as the announcement had ended, the lights in the room brightened and the clicks and whistles stopped, as if flipped off with a switch.

"And I was just starting to relax," Mrs. Sanders murmured, shaking her head. "Oh, well. Come on, now maybe we can get something to drink." Her face grew serious as the two of them went back the way they had come, and Kyle was pretty sure there was more that she wasn't saying.

Mrs. Sander picked up her coffee cup then set it down on the table again, finally looking up. "Kyle..." She tried to smile, then swallowed. "I'm not sure how to start this."

Kyle stayed silent as he took a drink from his smoothie. An awkward silence fell between them.

"All of this is just scaring me." Mrs. Sanders took a deep breath. "The note, the blackout. It just sounds so..." She trailed off, shaking her head. "Familiar. I thought they had forgotten about me," she muttered.

"Who forgot about us? Who's after us?!" He hadn't meant it to come out so forceful, and he winced.

Mrs. Sanders looked startled, then she picked her cup up again. "I can't say here. Maybe you'll understand someday."

Kyle considered asking her about the clerk, but this time he wasn't so sure he should. If she was keeping everything a secret from him, maybe he should have a secret of his own. Anyway, it seemed like she already knew who was after them. How could she think it was safer for him not to know?

"So what do we do?" he asked instead.

Mrs. Sanders looked up warily. "There's nothing we can do but wait. Once we get to land, we'll contact the police."

"So we're just going to run? My mom said that if you run away, your problems will just follow you."

"Your mom got herself *killed* facing her problems!"

Her words spread over him like ice. Without even thinking about it, he bolted out of his chair and ran toward the opening of the café. He didn't know where he was going. He just had to run somewhere. He had thought he could trust Mrs. Sanders, yet she was just like everyone else. Why did she have to hide everything? He realized his chest was heaving, and slowing to a stop, he sank against the wall, letting tears slide down his face. It was like Mrs. Sanders had torn open an old wound. All the pain and heartache he had felt when his parents had died was now coming out. He could hear his sobs echoing down the hallway, but he didn't care. He barely noticed when someone put a hand on his shoulder.

"Kyle? Are you okay?"

Kyle pulled away when he recognized the voice. *Beth*.

"Mind if I sit down?" Apparently, she took his silence as permission, and he heard her sit down next to him. "Life never really goes the way we want it to, does it?" It sounded more like a statement than a question.

Life definitely didn't go the way *he* wanted. If it did, he would still be with his parents, not on a cruise ship being hunted by someone he didn't even know, or worse, someone he did.

She put a hand on his shoulder again, and this time he didn't pull away. "I hate to see anyone go through hard situations. If there's anything I can do to help, don't hesitate to ask."

"I guess it's just been exciting with the blackout and everything else," he said, looking down at the carpet. He didn't really know why he said that.

"Yeah. I guess it has been," she replied, a smile in her voice. "Apparently, the fuel line to the generator got clogged. I guess stuff like that just happens. Last time, it was a blown cooling hose."

Kyle felt a jolt go down his spine, and looked up at her for the first time.

"What if it wasn't an accident?" He hadn't realized he'd said it out loud until Beth raised an eyebrow.

"Really?" A grin spread across her face. "That just sounds like a spy movie."

Kyle's heart raced and his mind flashed to his necklace. "What if someone wanted to break into a cabin and steal something?"

Beth frowned in thought, then slowly nodded. "I guess it would have disabled the cameras, and those locks aren't impossible to hack into. They are electronic, after all. And I guess security would be watching the shops." She quickly shook her head. "But why would someone go through that much trouble for some valuables? There are much easier ways to rob one of the stores."

He swallowed, still not sure if he should tell her about the strange note. The clogged hose sounded just as absurd. Taking a deep breath, he made up his mind.

"It might go with a note that we found in our cabin." He held his breath as Beth stared at him.

"What kind of note?" she asked, scrunching her eyebrows.

Kyle closed his eyes and took a deep breath again. "It said something like, 'your cover is blown. Get yourself and Kyle off the ship as soon as possible.' It was signed 'a friend.'"

"Kyle! Wha—?" Beth stared at him aghast. "Did you tell security yet? A threat like that is illegal!"

Kyle started. If it was illegal, then it wouldn't be a joke. The room suddenly felt cold, and he felt the urge to look behind him. Someone was definitely after him.

"Man," Beth murmured, still sounding shocked, "this is starting to look like a detective movie. Did you tell anyone else about the note? Your mom?"

"She doesn't care. All she wants to do is run!" He bit his lip, realizing he had shouted the last part.

"Isn't that what the note said to do? Kyle, if what you say is true, then anyone on this ship could be after you. You don't even know if you can trust security."

A bolt of fear ran through him. Hadn't they handed the note to the officer? What if he were the one chasing them? *No, then he would have just caught us there, when no one was around.*

"But you're right."

Kyle turned back to Beth, who was staring at the wall, a new look of determination in her eyes.

"If you want your problems to be over with, you have to face them." She turned to face him, looking him in the eyes. "Do you have any idea whom the note might be referring to?"

He tried to think through everyone he had met since leaving. There was Brianna, though she didn't seem likely. Although she *had* tried to drown him. Still, she didn't look like she could take on Mrs. Sanders. Then there was the clerk. "There's the clerk in the jewelry shop. He has a necklace exactly like—" He stopped, his face heating up.

Beth just looked at him, waiting for him to finish.

Kyle swallowed. "Exactly like one my mother had." He was surprised when she shook her head.

"Just because he has a replica doesn't mean it has anything to do with the note. Maybe we'll find the answer to that question if we figure out who wrote the note," Beth suggested. "We could go with your assistant. She would—"

This time, Kyle shook his head, cutting her off. "No. I saw a note she wrote. I'm pretty sure it's not the same handwriting."

Beth let out a breath, then stopped. A second later, he heard hurried footsteps and Mrs. Sanders appeared around a bend.

"There you are, Ky—"

She stopped when she saw Beth, narrowing her eyes. "And who are you?"

Beth got to her feet, smiling. "I'm Elizabeth Quigley, the speaker onboard the *Dolphin Diamond*. I just found him crying... I have three children. I just want you to know how amazing he is."

Mrs. Sanders' hard gaze softened a bit. "Sorry, it's just been a hard day."

Beth smiled knowingly. "Yeah. I guess it has been. Anyway, I've got to get back to my work. I need to rewrite the entire introduction for tomorrow's presentation. If you need someone to talk to, you can usually find me in the café." She gave one last wave to Kyle, winked, then hurried down the corridor toward the café.

When he turned back to Mrs. Sanders, he found her looking at him almost sadly.

"Kyle, I'm sorry. I shouldn't have said what I did. Your mom was a great woman, even more than you know…" She trailed off, and Kyle felt a lump form in his throat. She looked like she might say more, but instead she shook her head. "Come on. What do you say we go get an early dinner? I don't think a grilled cheese sandwich was really enough for lunch."

She was obviously hiding something. He was sure it had to do with the note. Why had the person written, "Your cover is blown"? It made it sound like Mrs. Sanders was a… Kyle stopped, and Mrs. Sanders turned to him, her weary face making her seem even more like a secret agent. *But that's impossible.* You couldn't just hide the fact that you were a secret agent, could you?

15

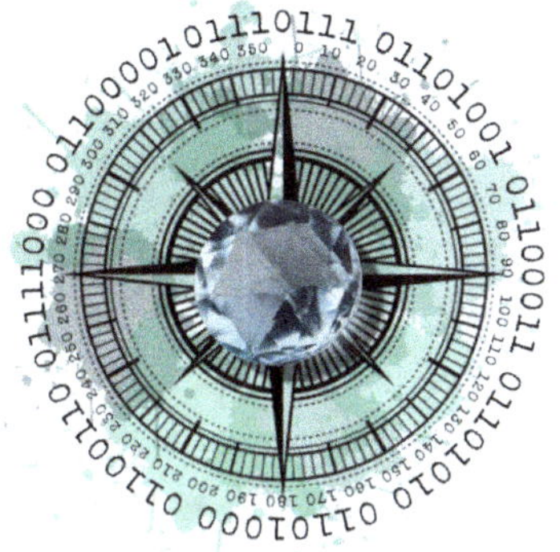

Kyle stared out the window, remembering how on the first day of the cruise he had imagined what it would be like when they were on the ocean. Now, they were there, and someone was chasing him. And the endless waves just added to the feeling of being trapped.

"All right. What would you like?" Mrs. Sanders asked. "There's pasta, soup, tacos, some meat dishes, and pizza. You could get the salmon omelette again," she teased, nudging him. Kyle looked up at her, his anger melting away into a mixture of fear and something else he couldn't place.

"I want this cruise to be over," he whispered, swallowing as a lump formed in his throat.

"Oh, Kyle..." Mrs. Sanders said, and he felt her wrap an arm around him. "I'm sorry. If I had known about any of this, we wouldn't have come."

"But you *do* know who's after us!" He suddenly couldn't keep his tears in any longer, and they rolled down his cheeks. "Why do you have to keep everything a secret?!"

"Kyle!" Mrs. Sanders said, taken aback. "Why would you think I know?"

He decided to take a shot in the dark. "Because you were with her. Because you said she killed herself trying to face her problems."

Mrs. Sanders froze, and Kyle knew he had hit something. Finally, she sighed, sitting down on her bed. "All right. I'll tell you as much as I can." She shook her head, closed her eyes, then started.

"Your mother and I both worked for a... research center called the Crystal. I joined the team as a cryptologist, someone who studies codes, and she joined as a marine biologist. At the time, she was working on a project about dolphin communication..."

She still seemed to be hiding something, and he briefly wondered what she was leaving out. Still, he hung onto every word. He had never really heard about his mother's work before.

"I met you when you were just a preschooler, maybe five," Mrs. Sanders continued. "Back then, you were so energetic and playful, and you never fussed. You always seemed happy, and you loved the dolphins. I worked with her for about five years, until the accident. We'd just had a breakthrough, and your mother started writing things down like crazy. She would spend all day working and all night in the boat, writing. When I asked her if she slept, she replied, 'Only with half of my brain!'" Mrs. Sanders gave a distant smile.

"Eventually, she got so tired that I forced her to take a vacation. Seven days away from her dolphins. She wasn't very happy about it, but she went anyway. You were ten then, and you hadn't seen her for weeks."

Kyle felt a sinking in his stomach as he realized where she was going with the story. He'd had nightmares about that one night hundreds of times.

"It was for that reason that she decided to go. She took you and your father. However, halfway through the vacation, we were warned about a tropical storm. We tried to get to you guys to warn you, but none of your radios were working. A day later, I heard that the *Emerald Wind* had been spotted wrecked on a beach, and a boy had been found in the wreckage. When they said you were up for adoption, I immediately put in paperwork for you. That was a few months after my husband and son died in a car accident, and I was lonely. I thought that maybe God had answered my prayers and sent you to me. I also thought that I owed it to Jill, so I adopted you. And that's the end of the story." She took her head.

"Or that *was* the end. Now, two years later, a note appears that says someone is after us. Kyle, you're old enough to know the truth. I think someone tampered with your radio on the ship, and I think the same person realized you didn't die."

A cold feeling swept over Kyle as he realized what she was saying. His parents' death hadn't been an accident. Someone had sabotaged the *Emerald Wind*. But who would do that, and why?

Tears welled up in his eyes.. Why did it still hurt so much when it had all been two years ago? Mrs. Sanders was silent for a long time. Finally, she spoke quietly.

"Kyle. I know how it feels. My husband and son died two years ago."

"Then why don't you act like it? Why can you and Ocean act like nothing happened, when it still hurts for me?" He hadn't realized he had said it out loud until he felt Mrs. Sanders clutch his hand.

"It still hurts, but I let go of my pain a while ago. You bottled yours up, and it only comes out when it's too much. Pain is like a slowly filling jar. If you keep it closed, it will fill up, then the pressure will build until the jar can't hold it anymore and it all comes rushing out. If you keep it closed, it will keep overflowing." She looked straight into his eyes. "You have to open it up and let it out. It's painful, but that's the only way it will heal."

"I can't," he whispered, biting his lip. "If I let it out, I'll forget about them, just like you forgot about your husband and son."

Mrs. Sanders sighed. "I haven't forgotten about them. I've just let the pain go. You won't ever forget about them, but you can still move on, Kyle."

He swallowed, knowing he couldn't let go of the pain. If he did, the memories would fade. The scene of the wave crashing over him flickered in his mind, and he swallowed again. Did he even want to remember them? "*How* do I let go of my pain?" he forced himself to ask, looking up at Mrs. Sanders, who smiled in return.

"Just tell me what happened the day they died."

His mind flashed back to that day and through everything that had happened since then. He couldn't stop the memories from flooding him, as usual, but this time the flashback was different.

"Kyle!" his mother screamed, wind whipping around her as a wave slammed into the boat and she lost her grip on the rope. He could see her grabbing frantically around, but he could also see the bed and Mrs. Sander's face. He watched as her head smacked against the railing, and she fell limp into the churning water. He

watched as time snapped forward and his father rushed into the wave, headed for the helm. He watched as the same wave turned the boat and he fell into the railing, going underwater. He felt the loneliness and fear he'd experienced as the cabin was jerked around, water filling it rapidly. He felt the shaking as the rocks tore at the hull, and then the jolt as the boat crashed onto the rocky shore. He felt the terror he'd had as he saw the officer, and the emptiness as he was led away and put in the back of the police car, the officer saying into his radio, "We found him. No sign of his parents, though."

He wanted to scream, "They're dead. They drowned!" But he couldn't.

"Kyle? What's happening? What happened?"

The words shocked him out of his nightmare, and he shrank away from Mrs. Sanders. Gradually, the fear disappeared and was replaced by a deep ache.

"They died. My mom" —he shook his head as tears streamed down his face— "hit her head and fell off the ship." He tried to say more, but he couldn't. His throat was too tight. Instead, he leaned into Mrs. Sanders, burying his head in her shirt as he cried.

After a while, his adoptive mom spoke. "Kyle, I'll always be here for you."

He didn't know how long he stayed like that, but it didn't seem to matter. Finally, he pulled away from her, wiping his eyes on his sleeve. He gazed out at the endless ocean, the trapped feeling closing in again. Someone on this ship was after them. *But why? For a necklace?*

"Kyle, I know this is hard," Mrs. Sanders said, wrapping an arm around him. "Maybe I'm wrong. Maybe it isn't someone's fault. I just wanted someone to blame..." She trailed off, shaking her head.

"What if God's the one to blame?" He shot back. "Why wasn't He there when they died?" God hadn't stopped his parents. He hadn't sent anyone to rescue them when they were in the storm.

He hadn't stopped them from leaving when He had known that they would die if they left. If God really existed, He didn't care enough to do anything, just like everyone else.

"Kyle," Mrs. Sanders said, kneeling down to look him in the face, "this isn't God's fault. He lets bad things happen because He lets us choose what we do. It isn't God's fault. It's mine." She bit her lip, glancing away from him. Kyle just sat there. He hadn't ever thought that it could be her fault. He hadn't even known she had told his mother to go on the trip until a few minutes ago.

"I was only looking out for her. I didn't know that...Kyle, I'm sorry. I didn't tell you...because I thought you would hate me. I needed you to love me." Her voice cracked, and a tear slid down her face.

Kyle blinked, not knowing what to do. He wanted to tell her that she hadn't killed his parents, but he couldn't. Part of him *wanted* to blame her.

"You only did what you thought you should do." He remembered what Ocean had said to her father. "You can't change the past."

Mrs. Sanders sighed. "Sometimes I wish I could. I wish I could have stopped them from getting in that car. I was supposed to be the one who died. I was supposed to drive Thomas to basketball camp, but my husband said I looked too tired. I was supposed to be on that boat, but at the last moment, I decided to let your mom have some alone time with her family." For the first time since he had met her two years ago, she looked defeated. "I'm sorry, Kyle. You're right. I can't fix the past. But I'm still responsible for their deaths."

"But if you had died, I wouldn't have had anyone." Kyle didn't really know why he said it. In the last few hours, he had found out that his adoptive mom was not only a secret agent but also being hunted. Was she really better than foster care? Part of him wanted to say no, but he couldn't stop himself from wondering what life would have been like if she hadn't adopted him.

"Kyle, are you alright?"

Kyle blinked, realizing he had just been staring into space. "I'm fine," he said quickly, shaking his head.

Mrs. Sanders sighed. "I know this must all be hard to take in. Maybe we could play a game to take our minds off it for a while." She hesitated a moment, then disappeared into the bathroom and came out a minute later holding two boxes, which she placed on the carpet. "All right. Chess or checkers?"

"I don't like games that much. My parents never really played any."

"Right. Well, then, what *do* you want to do?" she asked.

Kyle looked out the window. Without him realizing it, the last trickles of sunlight had slowly disappeared, and now the only light came from the ones overhead. Another day had passed. An odd sense of relief filled him and he realized he was tired.

"Maybe we could just go to bed."

Mrs. Sanders sighed. "I guess you're right. I honestly don't like chess all that much either." As she went to put the games away, Kyle looked back out at the ocean, but instead of water he saw himself looking back, reflected by the light inside the cabin. He was surprised at how tired he looked. Had it only been that day that they had found the note? It seemed like one moment everything had been fine. Then the next moment, everything had turned upside down.

Kyle stared up at the ceiling. He knew he should be sleeping right now, but the questions whirling around in his mind wouldn't let him. Everything was wrong. Why had Ocean been so angry when he talked to Haley? She must know deep down that Haley didn't really have a part in Brianna's bullying. And why had she let that come in between their friendship? Maybe Brianna was right. Maybe Ocean really was a deserter.

Kyle sighed into the darkness. What if *he* was the one who was wrong? Maybe if he would just apologize everything would be better. But apologize for what? The question kept coming back. Why was it wrong to talk to Haley?

He sighed again. Wondering wasn't going to get him anywhere. Then again, what else *could* he do? It wasn't like he could figure out who was after them. Or could he? Could it be as simple as the suspect being the clerk? Maybe all he had to do was tell security everything. *Hey, my mom's a secret agent—* Was she, though? There seemed to be something she was leaving out.

Sighing a third time, he settled down in his bed as the questions that had been flooding his brain since his talk with Mrs. Sanders resurfaced. If someone was after them, then *why*? His parents had been killed in a tropical storm, right? Then why had Mrs. Sanders looked like she was hiding the truth when she'd told him? Of course, that *was* the story everyone else had told too. The pastor, the coast guard, and the police had all said the same thing, that it was an accident, but what if only Mrs. Sanders knew the truth? Otherwise why had she said that the radio had been tampered with? Why had she said the same people who killed his parents were after him and Mrs. Sanders now? Why would they be after her if all she did was—what? What had she actually done on his mother's team? Had she told him?

He glanced over where she lay under her covers. What was she hiding and why? Had she even told the truth at all? Maybe whoever it was had killed his parents trying to get Mrs. Sanders. Slowly, he found himself thinking about the person who had sabotaged the ship. Too bad the note hadn't told them who *was* after them. But if someone wanted to kill him, why hadn't they done it yet? *Something just doesn't feel right about it. Someone sabotaged the boat. The blackout!* What if the person who had sabotaged the *Emerald Wind* were planning on sabotaging the cruise?

He rolled over, hoping he would just fall asleep. Nothing made sense. If someone was going to sabotage the ship, why wait until it was almost at the dock? He bolted upright. Of course! If he were going to sabotage a ship, he would want to get off before it sank. But it also meant everyone else could get off too. He sank back down, sighing. That meant he was back at square one.

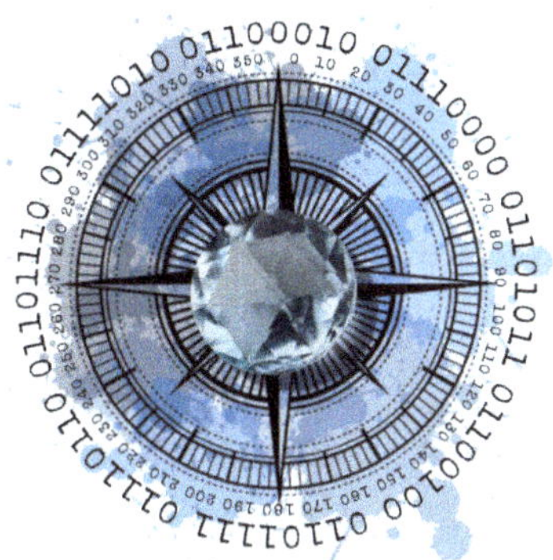

16

HE MUST HAVE FALLEN asleep, because the scent of strawberry pancakes was drifting through the room when he opened his eyes again. He squinted at the form of Mrs. Sanders standing above him.

"Good, you're awake! I went ahead and ordered us pancakes."

Something seemed off about her, but in the bright light he couldn't tell what. Groggily, he climbed out of bed, heading to the bathroom to change. After he had finished, he emerged to find Mrs. Sanders waiting for him, smiling. That's what was so weird! He hadn't seen her smiling since they had found the note. It was like she had completely forgotten about everything that had just happened.

"The pancakes are on the desk. Hurry up and eat. We have to leave in ten minutes."

Kyle sighed. Why couldn't she just wake him up with enough time to eat? Quickly he grabbed a plate, two pancakes, and a mini carton of milk from the desk. As he ate, he couldn't help glancing at his adoptive mom. She almost looked *too* happy. "Okay, what's going on?"

Mrs. Sanders just gave him one of her famous *I know and I'm not going to tell you* looks.

He was about to remind her of the note, but something stopped him. Mrs. Sanders was happy. Maybe the note could wait. Finally, he finished the pancakes and automatically looked for a sink to put his dishes in before his mind caught up.

"They'll clean it up when we're gone. Come on!" Mrs. Sanders opened the door, and Kyle followed her out into the soft glow of the hallway. Quickly, they made their way to the elevator, and Kyle briefly wondered if he should ask where they were going. He figured if Mrs. Sanders wanted him to know she would have told him, and judging by how mysterious she was being, it was probably a surprise. As they neared the elevator, however, she kept going forward, turning left at a new hallway where a scoreboard of some sort was hanging on the wall. They made their way over to the only door at the end where something like a vending machine sat next to a bin of golf clubs.

"Wait, we're going golfing?" he asked. *How would that work on a cruise ship?*

"No, silly, it's mini-golf. I figured since it's here on the cruise we might as well use it." She pressed a green button on the machine and scanned her wristband under a little crevice. A second later a green ball rolled into a little tray. "All right, your turn." She turned to him. "What color do you want?"

Kyle looked closer at the machine. Nine large buttons were embedded on the surface, each with a different colored slot ranging from red to black. Hesitantly he pressed the yellow button, then waited as he heard the ball roll through the machine. A second later a pink ball dropped into the tray.

"Well, *that's* odd," Mrs. Sanders remarked, hiding a laugh, and Kyle couldn't help grinning. "I guess it's not perfect. Oh, well, just try again."

After he had gotten the right ball and a golf club that felt the least awkward, he followed her into a room filled with people and little obstacle courses made of grass. However, it wasn't the course, but the huge floor-to-ceiling window that caught his attention.

"Why don't you go find a course that isn't full while I check us in," Mrs. Sanders suggested, already heading for the booth near the door.

Something still seems off about this whole thing, he thought as he searched the room for an empty course. There seemed to be people on every one. *And any of them could be watching us.* He shook the thought away as he squeezed his way through the crowd. Finally, he spotted an empty course near the back corner of the room. It just had a starting point, a hole, and what could only be described as a boulder field. *No wonder no one's here.*

Still, he waited there for Mrs. Sanders. A minute passed, and he tried to ignore the feeling that he was being watched. No one would attack them with so many people around, right? *What if someone's kidnapped Mrs. Sanders?*

Finally, he spotted her through the crowd, and his heart lifted. Then it fell again when he caught sight of Paul next to her and Ocean trailing behind, looking skeptical. As soon as Ocean saw Kyle, her skepticism turned into anger. *Great.* So that's what Mrs. Sanders had been planning. He tried to ignore Ocean as he focused on the course.

"It was Paul's idea." Mrs. Sanders said, grinning. She got a mischievous look. "You know, there's a course open near the door that doesn't look as hard. Maybe you two could try that one out. I want to see if I can beat the 'Master Mini-Golfer' over here." She winked at Paul. For a moment, Ocean's look mirrored Kyle's unease, then she scowled at her father.

"I don't like mini-golf."

He gave her a strange look. "You've been acting weird ever since you left the pool. Did something happen?"

Instead of answering, Ocean continued, "I never wanted to even come on this cruise!"

"Ocean! This isn't only about you! What's got into you?"

Without responding, Ocean suddenly took off through the crowd.

"Ocean!" Paul shouted after her. He sighed. "I'd better go after her."

The heavy weight of guilt rolled in Kyle's stomach, and without thinking about it he spoke up. "No, this is my fault." Without waiting for a response, he started in the direction Ocean had gone.

"Kyle!" Mrs. Sanders yelled, but he ignored her, pushing his way through the people toward the door. He barely caught sight of the telltale prosthetic disappearing behind the doorway. Finally, he emerged from the crowd and ran the rest of the way to the door. As he rounded the corner into the hallway, his heart sank. There was no one in sight. *Great.* Although, did he honestly want to talk to her? Maybe it was better that they weren't friends. Maybe he should just give up. He was about to turn around when he heard someone crying.

Cautiously, he walked down the hallway, and his heart felt like it was being squeezed. It was definitely Ocean. Everything in him wanted to turn around, but something stopped him. Before he could change his mind, he pushed open the oak double doors in front of him to find Ocean sitting against the wall, her face buried in her knees.

His stomach clenching, he started toward her, and she suddenly looked up, her eyes red. Kyle stopped, and for a moment, it seemed like she was about to spring up, then she looked away, fresh tears sliding down her face. Carefully, he walked toward her. After an awkward silence, he sat down next to her, his back against the cool wall. He stayed that way, picking at the maroon carpet, not sure what to do next.

"I'm sorry," Ocean whispered. "I just used to be fine with having no friends. I just—" Her voice cracked, and she looked down, fresh tears falling down her cheeks. "I miss my mom," she croaked out, then buried her face in her knees again.

"I miss her too." Just saying it out loud made it seem more real, and his throat tightened. Then he straightened, "*My* mom, not..."

Ocean let out a choked laugh. "Yeah, I got that." Then she fell silent again.

"Also, I'm sorry I challenged Brianna to the fight. I guess I just wanted her to stop bullying you." *There. I said it.*

Ocean snorted. "As if she would have stopped if you'd won. She breaks almost every promise she makes." She sighed. "I guess I'm sorry I got mad at you. You were right. Haley didn't have anything to do with it. She really just hangs out with the wrong friend."

Kyle decided not to tell her it was because Brianna didn't *have* any friends.

"So what do you think about your mom and my dad?"

He blinked at her, and she smirked, her old self returning.

"They definitely seem to be hanging out a lot together," she teased. "Why do you think they sent us to a different course?"

He suddenly felt queasy as he realized what Ocean was trying to say. "Maybe they're just friends."

Ocean's smile fell. "Maybe, but he's had a lot of 'friends' and they've never acted like your mom."

"We should head back," he said, trying to change the subject

Ocean just smirked, then got up and headed for the mini-golf area, wiping her face with the back of her hand. Kyle got up and followed her, feeling suddenly lighter. Maybe the rest of the cruise would go by smoothly and the notes *were* just an elaborate joke. Maybe Ocean lived near him, and they could still be friends after the cruise.

"Oh, and Kyle?" she asked suddenly, an edge to her voice.

"Yeah?"

"Don't look now, but I think someone's following us."

His heart leapt into his throat as he spun around. He was just in time to see a figure slip behind one of the doorways that branched off the hallway.

17

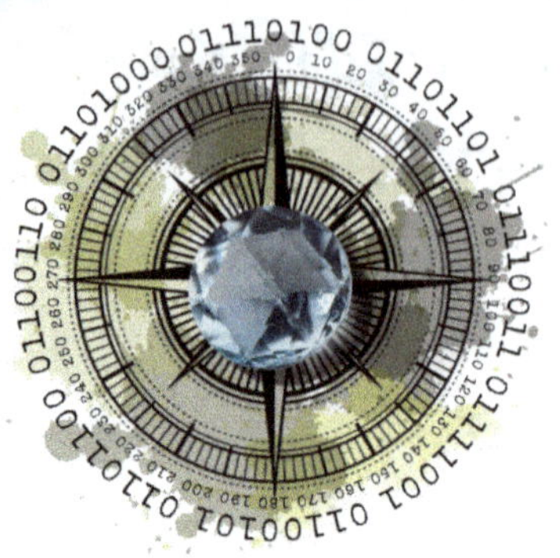

"ARE YOU SURE YOU saw someone following you?" Mrs. Sanders asked, anxiety clear in her voice.

Kyle looked down at their cabin carpet, swallowing. "I don't know. It was kind of hard to—"

"Definitely," Ocean interrupted, fear on her face. "What's happening? First you get a note, then the power goes out, and now someone's following us."

"I'm sorry. I shouldn't have gotten you involved," Mrs. Sanders replied, shaking her head. "You both need to leave."

"Hold on, we're—"

"Now!" She cringed. "I'm sorry. I don't want anyone else to get hurt because of me."

"What do you mean?" Kyle asked, a sense of dread forming in his gut. "You said you were working with my mom; how—"

This time, Paul held up a hand. "I don't know what happened, but I know you didn't hurt Kyle's parents. Sometimes you just have to accept that you don't have control of every-thing. And we're not giving up." It looked like he wanted to say more, but instead he just crossed his arms.

Sighing, Mrs. Sanders sat down on her bed. "Thank you. But I don't want to put you in danger."

"If your life is in danger, I'm not going to just stand to the side." He squeezed his eyes shut, then opened them. "Not again."

"So...what are we going to do?" Ocean cut in, and both she and her father looked at Mrs. Sanders.

"We need to get off this ship." Mrs. Sanders' words cut through the air, and Kyle felt the heat rising inside him again.

He couldn't help himself. "And then what? Just run away until they give up?"

"I don't know, Kyle. What else can we do?" Mrs. Sanders suddenly sounded old and tired. "You don't know who we're up against."

He wanted to ask, *"And you do?"* But something stopped him. Maybe she wasn't telling him for a reason. *Who had that figure been?* It had happened too fast for him to get a good look, but it had definitely appeared to be a female.

"So what do we do?" Paul asked.

"For now we just need to be alert. Then we need to figure out where to go. We *are* in the middle of the ocean, after all."

Just like my parents, Kyle thought, his stomach churning. Suddenly, the cruise seemed like a cage, and they were trapped with a lion.

"O KAY, RIGHT NOW WE'RE about 30 miles from the coast, which means there's no way to get to land." Mrs. Sanders was at her computer, looking at a map of the cruise ship's path. "However, the day after tomorrow we're supposed to dock at Marathon."

"Which means the person is going to strike before then."

Mrs. Sanders and Paul both turned to Ocean, caught off guard, and Kyle felt a chill run up his spine.

"Why do you say that?" Paul asked, giving her a hard stare.

Ocean didn't seem to notice. "Well, if someone is after you, the only reason they haven't struck yet is because they're playing with you."

"Ocean!" Paul snapped, but Mrs. Sanders held up her hand.

Ocean continued. "The blackout, the note...it's like a cat playing with a mouse before—"

"Ocean, that's it! Come with me!" Paul turned to Mrs. Sanders with an apologetic smile, but she didn't seem to notice. Kyle watched Paul as he marched his daughter out of the room.

"I should have seen it coming," Mrs. Sanders whispered. "They trapped us, again."

Kyle couldn't take it anymore. "*Who* trapped us? Why does everyone have to have so many secrets?"

"Kyle!" Mrs. Sanders suddenly snapped, startling him into silence. "I'm just trying to keep you safe!"

The hot anger inside him flowed to the surface. "No. You just want to run!" Suddenly, he couldn't stay in the cabin anymore. Without warning, he bolted to the door, running out into the corridor. He didn't know what he was running from, he just had to run. *Just like Mrs. Sanders.* At least *he* was trying to figure out who was chasing them. *Because she already knows.* So why wasn't she telling him? How did not knowing who was after them make him any safer? Tears welled up in his eyes, and he found he couldn't breathe. He slowed to a stop, pressing his back against the cool wall as the tears escaped, sliding down his face.

He let himself cry until the sound of footsteps forced him to stop. Still, he couldn't stand back up, and he prayed the person would just pass by. She didn't. After a moment, he heard Mrs. Sanders sigh and sit down next to him.

"I'm sorry, about all of this. And you're right."

Kyle looked up at her, blinking his tears away. Maybe he hadn't heard her right.

"I do want to run away. That's what fear does. It's what's always kept me alive. If I hadn't run, maybe I would have been able to save them, or at least I wouldn't have had to live with this guilt."

He felt a hand on his shoulder, and he forced himself not to shrug it off.

"Kyle, you're the only one I have left, and I'm going to do whatever it takes to keep you safe. But there's one thing I think you should know."

He looked up at her and was surprised to see her eyes were red. A pang of guilt went through him. She must have been crying too.

"Right before the accident, she told me that if anything ever happened to her, I should sell everything she had and put it in a trust fund for you."

Kyle nodded slowly. Mrs. Sanders had told him before.

"Everything except for the necklace. She said it was more precious than anything else she owned." Mrs. Sanders shook her head, and Kyle caught his breath, waiting. "It's just...the way she said it..." She trailed off, lost in thought.

That was it? His mother probably said it because it was carved by his father. It probably *was* more valuable to her than anything else. Maybe she knew it would be the most valuable thing to him too if she died. Suddenly, he wanted to hold it again, just to feel the smooth surface his father had carved.

Silently, he got up and headed back to the cabin, hearing his adoptive mom's footsteps behind him. Quickly, he slid his wrist over the lock, then pushed the door open, walking over to his drawer. Taking a deep breath, he opened it and took out the box. Was it lighter than before? Suddenly, he was afraid to open it. What if it was gone? *Why would it be gone? Why would someone want my necklace?* Taking a deep breath, he took the top off, revealing empty velvet padding.

He almost couldn't believe it. Frantically, he started digging around in the drawer, throwing out his new pajamas and notebook. It wasn't there.

"Oh, Kyle," Mrs. Sanders said, as if realizing something. "The necklace is in the desk drawer. I was just..."

Without waiting for her to finish, he ran over to the desk and opened the top drawer. There, on a pair of soft pajama pants, was the necklace, the polished wood of the dolphin shining in the light. He gently picked it up, then turned to Mrs. Sanders, heat flooding his face.

"I'm sorry. I should have told you. I was just thinking about what your mother said. What would make it so valuable? I know it's crazy." She placed a hand on his shoulder. "I know it's your necklace. How about this? From now on I won't touch it." He looked up and his anger melted when he saw the pain in her eyes.

He just nodded, fingering the little dolphin.

"Plus, if I don't stop touching it, I might be tempted to break it open."

Kyle's head snapped up.

"Relax. I'm just kidding." Although the way she said it made it sound like she was only *half* kidding. Maybe it would be better to hide it from her.

A beeping noise suddenly came from the bed, and Kyle's heart leaped into his throat. His first thought was "Bomb!" Then, as quickly as it had come, the beeping stopped.

Frowning, Mrs. Sanders walked over to the intercom, which now had a blinking orange light.

"I guess we have a message." She was about to press it, but she stopped, apparently thinking the same thing he was. What if it was another warning? Shaking her head, she pressed the button, and Kyle held his breath.

"Hi, Fiona, this is Paul."

Both Kyle and his mom let out their breath at the familiar voice, and he couldn't help grinning.

"I just wanted to let you know that Ocean has something for Kyle." Someone said something in the background. "Okay, pretend like I didn't say that. Apparently, Ocean wants you two to come to our cabin." Paul paused, and Kyle heard Ocean's voice again, though he couldn't tell what she was saying. "She said, 'Come alone. Bring no one. But his mom can come. Stop saying everything I'm telling you!' I think she's about to kill me. See you soon." There was a smirk in his voice as he ended the message.

"All right, then," Mrs. Sanders said, biting back a laugh. "Let's go see what all this is about."

18

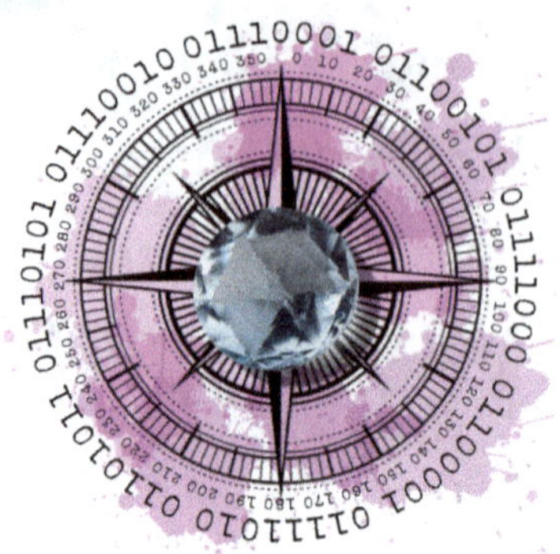

K YLE RAISED HIS HAND to knock, then hesitated. He had absolutely no idea what was on the other side of the door. Knowing Ocean, it could be anything. And he would be lying if he said the possibility that all this was a trap didn't cross his mind.

"Well?" Mrs. Sanders prodded from behind him.

Shaking himself, he knocked. There was no answer.

"That's odd..."

Kyle could hear the caution in her voice, and his heart quickened. Suddenly, the door opened and he did a double take. He had been expecting the unexpected, but what he hadn't expected was a normal-looking...birthday party? The entire room was decorated with gold streamers, and balloons with the words "Happy Birthday!" hung over a large wooden table. Obviously they were celebrating his birthday, but why?

"Bonjour, monsieur," Paul said, stepping out from behind the door, wearing a tuxedo, slicked-back hair, and a bow tie.

Kyle grinned. That part he had expected.

"*Ça vous plaît?*" Paul asked.

Kyle scrunched up his forehead. What did Paul mean by, "say to play," and why did he have a French accent?

"He's decided he's a French '*serveur*,'" Ocean explained, walking out from behind her father. "He asked if you like it."

Kyle just stared at her, and not because of her prosthetic this time. She was covered from head to toe in splotches of white. *Flour?*

"Okay, when I said—" Mrs. Sanders began, but the "serveur" cut her off.

"You like it? Oui? Wait. There is more." He disappeared into the kitchen, emerging a few seconds later balancing two metal trays piled high with pancakes, bacon and eggs, four glasses of juice, four vanilla ice creams, and a dozen slices of French toast.

"Your food, monsieur," he said, winking.

Kyle turned to stare at the food, and without warning, his stomach growled.

"Paul, you really shouldn't have," his mom said.

"I had to do something with the free food pass I got. Gotta give them a run for their money." Paul winked again, dropping his French accent for a second. "Now, *bon appétit*!" He gestured to a chair, and Kyle awkwardly sat down, followed by the others. He didn't know where to start.

Paul just grinned, then gave Mrs. Sanders a look. She nodded. He turned back to Kyle. "Happy Birthday!"

Kyle felt his face heating up as everyone turned to him, obviously expecting something.

"Uhh...thanks..."

"Your mom decided it would be nice to celebrate your birthday together," Paul continued.

"Okay..." he replied.

Kyle turned back to the food, trying to decide what to take first. Mrs. Sanders grabbed a pancake, and Kyle followed, taking a plate from the tray, then pouring maple syrup on it and dipping the pancake.

"Is that necklace new?" Ocean asked, suddenly.

He blinked, his hand automatically going to the lump in his shirt. His necklace was still there! How could he have forgotten about it again? Why hadn't he taken it off? "Yeah. I got it right before the cruise..." He stopped himself before he could say anymore.

"What does it look like?"

He looked back at her, and a thought struck him. He hadn't told her about the identical necklaces yet because he hadn't wanted to show her his mother's necklace. Was it selfish to keep the necklace hidden from her?

"I'm sure it's fine if he doesn't show you everything he has," her father pointed out, and Kyle breathed a sigh of relief. They finished eating in silence. As soon as they were done, Ocean hopped up from her seat, glancing at her father, who nodded.

Great. Another secret.

Without another word, she hurried to the kitchen, emerging a minute later holding the bluest cake Kyle had ever seen. *So that's why she's covered in flour!*

"*Pour vous, monsieur,*" she said, trying her best to sound French as she placed the cake on the table. "Look closely. I think you'll like it."

Kyle peered at it. The top had been whipped to look like waves and above, a pod of plas-tic dolphins was leaping out of the water behind a little yellow boat which Ocean probably got from some toy store onboard.

"It's beautiful," he said. How could he eat something she had probably spent hours on? Still, there was something off about it. "Where are the candles?"

Ocean and her father looked at each other.

"They didn't have any in the store," Paul began.

"So we just got this." Ocean pulled a glass candle out of a bag by her feet and placed it on the table. "It's birthday cake–scented, so we figured it was just as good."

"All right!" Paul announced, taking a golden lighter from his shirt pocket. "Let's light 'er up!" With that, he lit the candle.

"You'd better prepare yourself," Ocean whispered to Kyle. At the same time, Paul clapped and the lights went off. All Kyle could see was the candle and the light coming in through the window. Inwardly, he tensed. What were they planning?

Suddenly, accordion music started playing, and he looked around. He was surprised to see Ocean's father was holding the instrument.

"It is a tradition of ours to play 'Happy Birthday' on an accordion," he said in his most formal French accent. Then he started singing and everyone joined in, including Mrs. Sanders, and judging by the way she sang, she was finding it hard not to laugh.

"All right, now blow out the candle," Ocean said once they had finished.

Kyle took one last breath of cake-scented air, then blew. The little flame went out, and a cheer went up from Mrs. Sanders, Paul, and Ocean. Paul clapped again and the lights came back on, blinding Kyle.

"All right! Let's dig in!" Paul said, his French accent gone. He took a knife and carefully cut the cake, giving Kyle a piece on a glass plate.

After everyone had gotten a piece of cake, Kyle dug into his slice. The fork only went in a centimeter, then hit something hard. There was something inside. Carefully, he pulled the cake apart, revealing a paper envelope. *So that's the secret!*

Glancing at Ocean, who gave him a nod, he ripped it open and peered inside. His heart skipped a beat and he blinked, trying to clear his mind. There, sitting in the envelope, was a dolphin necklace, the same one from the shop.

"What's wrong? You looked really interested in it at the jewelry shop, so I decided to get it for you."

A thousand thoughts raced through his mind. If the clerk sold the necklace, he couldn't be the one trying to get *Kyle's*. That meant that someone else was chasing him, and he had no idea who or why. Shaking away his thoughts, he looked over at

Ocean, then Mrs. Sanders, who seemed to have a knowing look on her face. She nodded and he turned back to Ocean, wiping the cake and frosting off his hands and pulling his own dolphin necklace out so she could see it.

Her eyes widened and she looked from the envelope to his necklace, then laughed. "Well, now you have two of them."

Carefully, he took the new necklace out of the envelope, then took his old one off to compare it. Putting them side by side, he could easily see the difference. The necklace Ocean had given him was smooth and almost flawless, with intricate carved fins and a tiny dolphin-like grin on its rostrum. His mom's necklace was a lot more rugged, as if a large rough hand had carved it, and it had that one small knot on its tail.

"It was my mother's necklace," he said quietly as he spun it in his hand. "My father carved it for her as a wedding gift."

"Oh." Ocean's voice carried a hint of sympathy. "I guess you like it better, then."

"No, it's—" He searched for something to say that wouldn't hurt her feelings. "They're both special. I—"

"Attention!" a voice boomed from a speaker. Reflexively, Kyle spun toward the noise and felt his wrist whack into the table, his mother's necklace flying out of his grip. He barely had time to gasp before it hit the side of the counter and shattered.

19

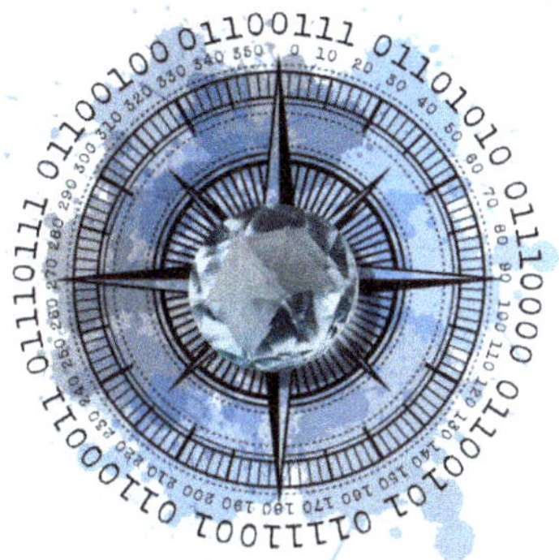

HEART POUNDING, KYLE STARED at the two pieces of wood lying on the carpet, ignoring the rest of the announcement. His mother's necklace was broken. The only thing he had left of her was now ruined. Carefully, he picked the pieces up, his tears making it impossible to see them clearly. One small mistake was all it took.

"I'm so sorry..." Ocean whispered. For a moment, no one spoke.

"Uh, Kyle?" she said louder.

Kyle blinked, looking up at her confused expression.

"I don't think it's broken."

He wiped away the tears as Ocean took the necklace from his hand and fit the two pieces back together. It looked completely fine. Furrowing her eyebrows, she pulled the pieces apart again.

"Hold on. There's a slot inside and it looks like something's wedged in it."

Kyle's mind flashed with questions. Had his mother left something else for him? Was he even supposed to have the necklace?

Carefully, Ocean picked at the object, finally getting a grip and pulling it free.

Kyle came up beside her as she held up the tiny chip, squinting at it.

"It's a micro SD card." She turned to him questioningly. "Perhaps—"

She was cut off by Mrs. Sanders' coughing. Kyle turned to his adoptive mom.

"It couldn't be—" Mrs. Sanders coughed, grabbing the card and sitting down in one of the seats.

"Fiona—" Paul began, but she cut him off.

"I'm sorry. I should have told you."

"Told us about what?" His eyes narrowed in confusion.

Mrs. Sanders looked down, then back up at him, and Kyle shifted awkwardly. She shook her head. "About the necklace. About the person who—" She glanced at Kyle, catching herself. "About everything."

Paul glanced at Ocean, then gave Mrs. Sanders a hard stare. "Okay. Tell us now."

A look of realization and fear crossed her face, and Kyle felt his stomach drop.

"They're after the card," she whispered. "Kyle, come on." Her voice turned harsh as she got up and headed for the door. Heart now pounding, he followed after her, glancing from Ocean and her father, standing there, to his adoptive mom.

"Where are we going?" he finally asked as Mrs. Sanders hurried into the hallway, headed toward the elevator.

"We're going to our cabin." Her voice left no room for any objections. She kept walking briskly until they reached the elevator. Only when they were inside did she let out a breath. Slowly, the elevator descended, and she tensed as it neared their floor.

When the doors opened, she hurried over to their cabin, scanning her bracelet before leading Kyle inside and shutting the door quickly behind her. Somehow the room seemed more like a fort now, and he was a bit glad that it had a lock. Glancing back at Mrs. Sanders, now sitting on a bed, he realized he was shaking.

"How long are we going to stay here?" Unease crept up his spine.

"Either until security catches the person or we reach Marathon."

His mind flashed back to two days ago when she had announced they were headed to Marathon. Back when he hadn't known about the note or the person. Back then, the cruise had seemed like a dream. Now, it was more like a nightmare and he just wanted to wake up. Slowly, his mind drifted to the SD card. What could be on it that would make someone chase them? Did Mrs. Sanders know? He turned to her, but she was lost in thought and he decided against asking.

A knock at the door startled him, and Mrs. Sanders snapped out of her daze, her eyes narrowing.

"Anyone in here?" Paul's voice filtered through the door and she relaxed, walking over and opening it to reveal Paul standing there with Ocean, a laptop in his hand. "I figured we should see what's on that card. And you kind of left us hanging back there."

Slowly, she nodded, then let them into the room, shutting the door behind them. Paul slid into the desk chair, opening the laptop and turning it on. He logged in, then turned to face her, holding out his hand. Reluctantly, she handed him the card and he inserted it into a larger card, putting that into a slot in the computer. Kyle crept closer as a file browser popped up, showing one lone file with a lock on it.

Paul frowned. "Looks like it's encrypted. We'll have to hack into it."

"Couldn't that break the file?" Mrs. Sanders asked.

"Probably not. Most likely it's standard encryption and we just have to let the computer guess the password..." He trailed off as he pulled up a new window and started typing furiously. Finally, after a few moments, a list of numbers and letters started scrolling across the screen, and he turned around to face her. "Now, tell me about everything that's happened."

She brushed her hair back and sighed. "Where should I start?"

"I always start a story at the beginning." He grinned at her and she smiled tightly back.

"All right." She took a deep breath, then let it out. "It started with—" She stopped, glancing at Kyle, then continued, "my coworker's death." Even though he had heard it before, a stab of pain shot through him, like an old wound was being cut open again. He couldn't help tuning her out as she told the story again. Absently, he watched the numbers and letters scroll across the screen. When would the computer find the right ones?

"No, actually, I guess it started when I joined her team. I was working for a top secret organization as a cryptologist. I was assigned to work with Jill on a project about dolphin communication. Or that's what we told everyone. In reality, neither of us actually had a clue about how dolphins communicate. What we were really working on I've sworn never to reveal."

So *that* was what she had been hiding! All this time, he'd been told his mother was a marine biologist. Now both she and Mrs. Sanders were secret agents? How much of his life had been a lie?

"The part about her being a marine biologist wasn't a lie," she continued, seeing Kyle's confusion. "We were actually studying dolphins, just in case someone dug into our case. We thought we pretty much had a bulletproof cover."

She sighed. "So we got careless. We started talking about our project in public, always in code, of course. I guess someone figured out the code, though. We started noticing we were being followed. So we decided to split up and act like the job was finished. We even faked a breakthrough and then we went our separate ways." She wiped her eyes.

"Jill went on a vacation with her family, and I disappeared, living like a homeless person. Really, I think she had it better." Mrs. Sanders smiled sadly. "The rest is kind of a mystery. Officially, Jill and her family sailed into a tropical storm and the boat wrecked, but I kept asking myself why they weren't warned about it. They had a ship radio, an emergency radio, and a handheld. For all three of them to fail, not to mention the barometer..." She trailed off, a distant look on her face. "It just doesn't make sense."

Without warning, Kyle's mind flashed to a scene right before the storm.

"Jill, you're not going to like this!" his father called out. Cautiously, Kyle crept toward the navigation room just as his mother entered the cabin. She caught his eyes, then motioned for him to follow her as she headed toward Father. A wave slapped the boat as he entered the room, sending him stumbling into his father, who caught him.

"What's going on? Greg?" Mom asked, coming up beside him.

"I don't know."

Kyle looked up at the dials, all of which were spinning in circles as his father continued, "Either the boat is spinning or the gauges are broken. I've tried the radio, but there's been no answer."

A look of concern and confusion flooded Mother's face, then her eyes lit up, a mixture of fear and realization. She had known, just like Mrs. Sanders had known where the note had come from.

"Kyle, are you okay?" Paul asked, and Kyle looked up at Mrs. Sanders.

"She knew," he said quietly. "My mother knew that the boat had been sabotaged."

Mrs. Sanders' eyes grew wide. "She took it with her," she whispered. "Right before we split up, she took the SD card that had all the research on it. I didn't see it after that. She said she had sent it to the police." She shook her head. "I should have known. She never trusted the authorities. I could have stopped—"

"No." Paul's voice was firm. "You couldn't have changed this any more than I could have saved my wife. I could have been there for her more. Then, maybe, she wouldn't have sailed away. But we can't control others, and sometimes, things are out of our control." A ding from the computer distracted him, and he turned back to it, frowning. "And this is one of those things. Apparently, her password doesn't match any of the top thousand. Which means it could take a few days to crack."

KYLE STARED UP AT the ceiling, knowing there was no way he was sleeping. The room he had thought of as a fort seemed more like a prison. One more day on the ocean and they would be at Marathon. Then what? Would the person stop chasing them when they got off the ship or would they spend the next few years running?

"You can't run away from your problems. They'll always come back stronger. But if you face them, they'll be gone for good." His mother's voice rang through his mind. They couldn't just keep running. Why couldn't his adoptive mom see that? They had to face the problem. If he stopped running, no one could chase him. Whatever the mysterious person had in mind, it was easier to handle than constantly running. And if he wanted to stop running, he had to do it tonight, before they reached Marathon.

Kyle looked toward Mrs. Sanders and was surprised to see her head tilted back, mouth hanging open. She had fallen asleep in front of the laptop. Carefully he slipped out of the covers and onto the soft carpet, slowly walking towards the door. Mrs. Sanders moaned and Kyle froze, heat flooding through him. Glancing at her, he breathed a sigh of relief. She was still asleep. Painstakingly, he grabbed the handle and turned it, slowly opening the door. With one last glance at Mrs. Sanders, he slipped out into the hallway, closing the door behind him. A smile spread across his face. He had broken out of jail.

Not caring as much about being quiet, he hurried through the hallway, then stopped. Where was he even going? Looking around, he realized he had automatically headed for the elevator.

Where could he go for help? Security would just bring him back to his room. That left Ocean and Beth. It felt weird talking to Beth about something so big. Still, Ocean was probably sleeping. He could at least *check* the café. With renewed purpose, he headed into the elevator, pushing the button for the top floor. A few moments later, he stepped out into the small carpeted lobby and headed for the café.

Even before he had reached it, he could tell that it was still open by the light filtering through the small aquariums lining the little room. He crept to the edge of the doorway and peered inside. The café was empty except for one lone table  where a lady worked at her laptop, sipping a coffee. *Beth*. His heart beat faster as he stepped through the doorway, making up his mind before he could second-guess himself.

Beth looked up with a tired, annoyed expression as he approached the table, but as soon as she saw him, she broke into a warm smile. "Kyle! How are you?" The implied *why are you here* was obvious in her voice.

"I just..." *Don't trust anyone.* "I'm fine. I just can't sleep."

"Still the note, huh?" She took a sip of her coffee. "Guess you could say the same for me–I can't sleep either until I figure out how to open the presentation. Openings are always so hard! Enough about me, though. Did you figure anything else out? Any idea who could be after you?"

Slowly, Kyle shook his head. "I know it's not the jewelry clerk."

Beth raised an eyebrow. "Oh?"

"Yeah, he doesn't have the other necklace anymore. I do. It's a long story," Kyle added when she cocked her head.

She nodded. "All right. Have you figured out why someone would be after you? That could help."

Kyle took a deep breath. If they were going to solve this mystery, he had to tell her. "Someone's after my mother's necklace."

Beth frowned. "You just said it—"

"It's not the clerk. Someone else is after it."

"Alright..." she said slowly, mulling it over. "Do you have any idea why?"

"I—" he stopped. He knew she only wanted to help, but he couldn't help wondering, what if *she* was the one the note was warning about. "I think it has something to do with my mom."

Beth nodded, though she seemed to be lost in thought. "What doesn't make sense is why the person hasn't just taken it already. Unless…"

"Unless *what*?" Kyle's heart started racing.

"Unless they don't know where it is or can't get to it." She looked at him, an idea forming in her eyes. "If you're right and they're after the necklace, then all we have to do is hide the necklace where they can't find it."

"I'm sorry, but the café is closing."

Kyle jumped at the new voice, turning to see a girl who looked about 16 wearing a brown cap and apron.

"Right," Beth said. "We were just about to leave. I need to escort him back to his room. He shouldn't be alone on the ship at night."

"I'm afraid I can't let you take him, as you know fully well. You didn't come in with him, and I'm pretty sure your wristbands aren't linked."

Beth scowled and seemed about to argue, but the girl cut her off.

"Of course, I could always call security to check. Pretty sure that would involve waking up the captain, though." The girl grinned as Beth's scowl deepened. "You could always help wipe down the tables, though."

"I'm sorry. I was just trying to help him." With that, Beth turned and marched out of the café, leaving Kyle alone with the girl.

"There's something off about her..." she muttered to herself, taking a rag and wiping down the table he was sitting at. She picked up Beth's empty coffee cup. "And she left her trash behind. Never a good sign." Turning to Kyle, she grinned. "Here." She tossed Kyle a spare wet rag. "You can wipe down the chairs. Oh, and my name's Quin, and we have a lot to talk about, starting with the fact that I wrote the note."

20

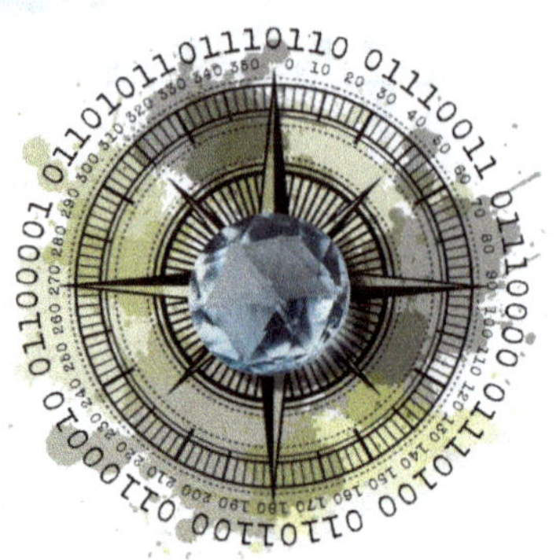

"Wait, what?!" Kyle could barely comprehend what she had just said. "What do you mean you wrote the note?"

The teenager, Quin apparently, sighed. "Kyle, please don't take it the wrong way, but everything I wrote is true. Someone is following you. At first—"

"You're the one who wrote the note?!" Kyle asked, incredulous. "You're the one who ruined the cruise?"

She recoiled and her eyebrows wrinkled. "No. Kyle, wait, I only—"

"You're the reason Ocean stopped being my friend? Why my mom is so worried?" Kyle cut her off again, barely listening.

"Kyle! Someone *is* chasing you. Someone is after something you have."

"How do you know? How do you know any of this?!" he snapped. All the fear that had been building up burst out of him. "What if you're the one who's chasing me?"

She looked him in the eyes, her face stern. "You have to trust me, Kyle."

A thought suddenly occurred to him. "How do you know my name?" He was sure he hadn't told her.

Quin blinked. "I just..." She trailed off. "You just have to trust me."

How could he trust her when she apparently knew everything about him? He narrowed his eyes at her. "Aren't *you* a stranger?"

"True," she admitted. "I could take you down to security *now*. But these tables need to get wiped down and I won't argue with having an extra two hands to help. We're down a barista."

Cautiously, Kyle picked up the rag, making sure to keep an eye on the exit. He knew he probably couldn't outrun her, but maybe he could at least scream for help. Beth was probably still nearby.

"I heard everything you said to Elizabeth," she continued. "If someone's after that necklace, you can't be giving it to random strangers."

"She's not a random stranger!" Kyle couldn't help raising his voice. "She's the only one who's helping me!"

"What about Mrs. Sanders? All she's trying to do is—"

"Run! All she's—" He stopped, narrowing his eyes again. "How do you know everything about me?"

Quin hesitated just a moment before continuing to wipe the table. "I don't know *everything* about you. I just know what I've seen and heard." She sighed. "I don't want to hide anything from you, Kyle."

"Just like my mom doesn't want to. What if *you're* the one who's after the necklace?"

A grin broke across her face. "Then I could just take it now. I know you're wearing it, just like Elizabeth did. But you know I'm not the one."

"How do you know that?" Though it was true. There was something about her that made him want to trust her. Still, she certainly *acted* like a spy. Kyle turned his attention to the rag as he ran it over a chair. Taking a deep breath, he asked the question that had been on his mind since he had first seen the note. "Then who *is* chasing us?"

Quin stopped scrubbing and turned to face him. "I don't know. You need to help me on that one. But first, you have to trust me. Do you think you can do that?" Her serious look made Kyle uneasy, and he glanced at the floor. Without thinking about it, he looked back up and nodded. He knew it was crazy, but deep down, he could tell that what she was saying was true.

"Good." She stood up and smiled. "Then we're going to do a trust fall."

Kyle squinted at her, confused. "A what?"

"A trust fall. You turn around and fall backward and trust that I'll catch you. If you don't trust me to catch you, how can you trust me to protect you?"

"Okay..." he said, though his heart was pounding. Slowly, he turned his back to Quin. Did he really trust her enough to not let him fall? *Don't let her drop me.* He wasn't exactly sure whom he was asking. God, maybe? With that, he let himself fall backwards, fighting the urge to catch himself. The room tilted, and he shut his eyes. Panic gripped him, and he twisted around, bracing himself. But instead of the floor, strong arms caught him, setting him back upright.

"Good enough." Quin smiled at him as his heart started to calm down. Why had he prayed she wouldn't drop him? When had God ever helped him? Where had He been when Kyle's parents had died?

"Kyle?"

He blinked, focusing on her concerned face.

"You don't have to help me now. We could wait a bit."

He shook his head, taking a deep breath. "No. We have to find the person before we dock."

Quin nodded. "Okay, who do you think would have a reason to be chasing you?"

He had been asked that question two times already. *You, maybe?* "I don't know. I thought it was the jewelry clerk, but he sold the necklace."

Quin frowned, taking out a notepad and writing something down. "All right. What do you think the person wants from you? What motive would they have?"

Kyle's mind flashed back to Mrs. Sanders' story. "I thought you heard everything we say?"

"Not everything. I only spy on you when you can't notice me. Why?" She returned to scrubbing down the table, and Kyle started on the chairs again.

"No reason," he said quickly.

Her only response was to glare at him.

"Why should I tell you anything?" he demanded.

"I thought you just said you trusted me."

"Why should I trust you?"

"Fine. We think there's something on an SD card inside the necklace. We're pretty sure that the information on it belongs to whoever's behind this, but we aren't positive. However, we don't actually know *who* was sent to retrieve the SD card. In fact, we didn't even know about the SD card—"

"What do you mean 'we'?" Kyle demanded.

"The Crystal. The academy your mother and Mrs. Sanders worked for."

Kyle just nodded, though a thousand questions were racing through his head.

"Keep in mind that the people we're dealing with also send kids to do missions, especially missions like this."

Kyle's eyes widened. Could Brianna be trying to get the card? Something about it didn't seem right. She seemed more like she just wanted to be better than anyone, although she *did* try to drown him. "Could Brianna and Haley be..." *What? Agents?* "What is the group that's trying to get the necklace?"

"I didn't say they *were* the ones, but they're an organization that wants power. They go under the name Rose Academy for the Excellence of Learning, but we just call them the Rose. They're basically a spy-training boarding school, like the ones in the books and movies, just a lot more political and twisted." Quin finished scrubbing the table, then looked around the café. Kyle followed suit, realizing they had finished the last table.

"All right. Time to bring you back to your room. We *are* being watched, after all."

He looked up, noticing the security cameras for the first time. Quickly, he followed her to the counter, where she put the rags in a bucket. Then she headed for the exit, Kyle in tow.

"We'll figure out who wants the SD card in the morning. Just come to the café with Ocean."

"What about Mrs. Sanders and Ocean's father?" Kyle asked. It was still weird that this girl knew everyone.

Quin looked down at the floor. "I don't think Mrs. Sanders would want to see me."

"But you said…"

"I said she was trying to help you. She doesn't know I'm here, and I think it should stay that way."

"What about Ocean's father, then?"

They were almost at his cabin now. Quin hesitated. "We should keep it between the three of us. The more people who know, the more likely it will be to spread." She paused as they reached door 71. "Also, adults can be stubborn. It's best to make this as easy as possible." With a nod, she headed away and Kyle scanned his wristband, opening his door to the bright light of his cabin. He let the door close behind him, remembering to be quiet too late. He winced at the sound and glanced at Mrs. Sanders, who was still sitting up in the chair, stretching.

"Oh man…" She yawned, shaking her head. "I should not have done that." Turning toward him, she started. "Oh, Kyle, what are you doing up? What time is it?"

Looking around, he spotted the alarm clock on the desk. It was 10:23 p.m. How was he going to explain why he was still awake?

"I just didn't want to wake you up."

"Oh. Sorry," Mrs. Sanders said, sounding a little guilty. "I guess we'd both better get to bed."

Luckily, she didn't ask what he had been doing. Of course that didn't mean she wouldn't. Quickly, he grabbed his pajamas from the wardrobe and hurried into the bathroom to change. As soon as he had finished brushing his teeth, he slipped out of the bathroom and into his bed.

Who was really after them? Why was Quin so wary about meeting Mrs. Sanders? It seemed like the more he learned the less he knew. At least tomorrow, he might figure out the answer to one of those questions.

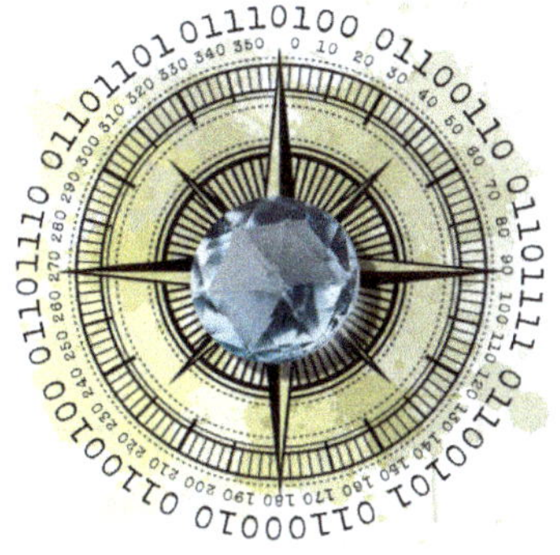

21

"KY, DO YOU SEE those stars over there?"

Kyle looked up at the sky. There were millions of stars. How could he see which ones Father was pointing to?

"Look for the brightest one."

Kyle scanned the darkness, settling on a bright red light. "You mean the big red one?"

Father laughed and tickled him. "Kyle, silly, that's Jupiter. It's a planet, not a star. The one you're looking for is white."

Kyle looked again, finally finding the star after many failed tries.

"All right, now, try to look for a big ladle made of stars. That star you see is part of the handle."

He quickly found the shape, though it looked more like a box with a handle.

"All right. Now find the bigger ladle."

There's a bigger one? *The one he had found was already huge. Searching the sky, he finally found it. It was so huge that part of it disappeared into the sea.*

"That star is called the North Star. As long as you sail toward it, you'll be sailing north. If you ever get lost at sea, Ky, and your gauges fail, you can always trust the North Star to guide you to land."

Kyle knew what was coming next.

"God is like the North Star. No matter how far you are from Him, you only need to follow Him to find your way back home. Let's see..." *Father reached under the ship's bench and pulled out the Bible he always kept there. Paging through it, he paused at a section and read.* "Jeremiah 23:13, 'You will seek me and find me, when you seek me with all your heart.'" *He flipped through some more pages, but Kyle stopped him.*

"What if I'm so far away I can't see the star?"

Father laughed. "Then I guess follow a compass. But if you lose sight of God, you can always follow His voice." *He held the Bible up.* "Even when we can't see Him, we can follow His voice."

The dream faded as light hit Kyle's face, and he opened his eyes, squinting at the window. He could still hear his father's words in his head. *"Even when we can't see Him, we can follow His voice."* But what if he couldn't hear God's voice?

Pushing his thoughts away, he slipped out of bed and glanced around. The window cast soft yellow light through the room. He turned to Mrs. Sanders to see if maybe she was awake, and he was slightly disappointed to see her covers rising and falling slowly.

Quietly, he walked over to the window, gazing out at the sparkling water. Something about the dream still clung to him. Why *had* he stopped following God? Father had said that if he followed God, he would find his way home, but where *was* home? And why had God led them into a storm? It didn't make sense, unless He didn't care.

Something in the ocean distracted Kyle from his thoughts, and he squinted at the water. Maybe it had just been a wave. *There!* A lone shiny gray fin cut through the surface, then disappeared. He caught his breath, almost not believing what he was seeing. Three more fins sliced the surface. *Dolphins.* One of them leapt out of the water, and for a moment he saw its torpedo-shaped body hang in midair before it fell into the ocean. Then, just like that, they were gone. For a moment, he scanned the water, trying to spot them again, but all he saw were the endless sparkling waves.

Why did dolphins always have to come and go so quickly? Just like his parents, they came, and then were gone. It happened so quickly.

Taking a shaky breath, he headed over to the dresser and picked out an outfit, then headed into the bathroom to change. When he stepped into the main room again, Mrs. Sanders was standing by the window. She turned toward him as he entered and smiled.

"You're up early," she remarked, crossing the room to him, then hesitating before squeezing his shoulder. "Breakfast should be here soon."

His heart skipped a beat, as he suddenly remembered the conversation with Quin last night.

"What is it?" Mrs. Sanders asked. "Is something wrong?"

He carefully thought over his words before responding. "I was planning on eating breakfast with Ocean."

She blinked, caught off guard, then she narrowed her eyes. "And where exactly did you two want to meet?"

"At the café." He waited as she pressed her lips together.

"Is Paul going to be with you?"

He hesitated, and Mrs. Sanders narrowed her eyes again. "She does know you're planning to have breakfast together, right?"

"Yeah." He stared at the carpet, his face burning. She sighed, and he knew she saw through his lie.

"Kyle, we can't keep doing this. We need to trust each other. We can't keep lying."

"Why don't you start then?" Kyle shot back, guilt and anger rushing into him at the same time.

"All right." She closed her eyes, took a deep breath, then opened them again. "Paul and I...are kind of dating."

Time seemed to freeze around them. He hadn't expected that.

"When my husband died, it was like part of me died too. I just never could fill the gap where he had been. I don't expect you to understand this, but there's something about Paul. When we're together, it's like the empty scar that my husband's death left starts to heal." Apparently, she saw the look on his face. "I'm sorry, Kyle. We're not getting married. Neither of us are ready. I just wanted to be honest. When all this is over..." She trailed off, swallowing.

Kyle suddenly understood why, and it made him sick. If he and Mrs. Sanders got away, the person chasing them would keep coming after them. They would have to move, maybe even join the Witness Protection Program.

"What do you say we grab Ocean and Paul and get some breakfast at the café?" She tried to put on a smile, but her eyes didn't have their usual sparkle.

Silently, he nodded. A few minutes later, they were knocking on Ocean's door. Paul answered, looking groggy, though as soon as he saw them, he brightened.

"What are you two doing here?"

Behind him, Kyle could see Ocean sitting on her bed in her pajamas. Something was off about her. It took a minute to realize what it was. She only had one leg. Her prosthetic was lying next to the bed. He instinctively turned away. Hopefully she hadn't noticed.

"...If it's okay with Ocean."

Kyle turned his attention back to Paul.

"Ocean, you up for eating with the fish?"

Ocean gave her father a confused look, and he grinned.

"Yep. We're game. Just give us a minute to get ready." With that, he closed the door.

An awkward silence filled the hallway, and Kyle stared at the floor.

"So now it's your turn. Why did you want to go to the café?"

He should have seen it coming. *We can't keep lying.* He took a deep breath. So much for not getting the adults involved. "Quin wants to meet us."

"Quin?" Mrs. Sanders looked puzzled, then she seemed to realize something. "The girl with the brown hair and way too much self-confidence?"

Kyle wondered if maybe it hadn't been such a good idea to tell her. "I guess so. She said you met before."

"What's she doing on this cruise? She's not even allowed to do missions yet." Mrs. Sanders' eyes widened. "I should have known! The handwriting."

"Who is she?"

"She was a student of mine, back when I taught writing and code breaking at the academy."

Kyle just stared at her. "What—" He was interrupted by the click of the door opening and Paul and Ocean stepped out of the room. Kyle was relieved to see Ocean was wearing her prosthetic.

"All right! Lead onward!" Paul proclaimed.

Mrs. Sanders looked like she might say something, then she shook her head, heading for the elevator.

Somehow, her knowing about Quin calmed Kyle. At least that was one less person that could be after the necklace. *The necklace!* He felt around his neck. It was still there. Why hadn't he taken it off? In fact, he hadn't taken it off for the past two days. Part of him knew why. Ever since he had learned someone was after it, he couldn't bear not having it with him. What if someone stole it from his room? Of course, wearing it meant to whoever was after it would go after him.

"Uh, Kyle? Are you okay?"

Ocean's voice startled him, and he dropped his hand "Y-yeah." *Why did I stutter?*

"Really? Then look behind you."

Kyle turned around to see Mrs. Sanders and Paul standing at the elevator. He had walked right past it! Quickly, he rejoined them, his face burning. The ride up was silent, which might have been worse than Mrs. Sanders chiding him. Finally, they arrived at the large elevator room. Kyle stepped out as soon as the doors opened, heading toward the café entrance.

"So, what *are* we doing?" Ocean asked, coming up behind him.

"What do you mean?"

"You act like you're going to a rendezvous site, not breakfast. Either that or you *really* like food all of a sudden." She turned to face him, walking backwards. "So what's going on?"

"You're not going to look where you're going?"

"I don't need to. You'll tell me if I'm going to hit something." She smirked, then spun around, coming beside him again. "So who are we meeting?"

Kyle blinked. She was pretty good. He decided to go with the truth. "Her name's Quin. And she seems to be helping us."

Both of them slowed as they neared the café entrance. Taking a deep breath, Kyle stepped through the opening and jumped back when he saw Quin a few feet away, watching them intently.

"There you two are!" she exclaimed as soon as Ocean came up beside him, "You're late!" Tossing them two aprons, she grabbed their hands and led them behind the counter, toward the kitchen.

"Not so fast, Quin." Mrs. Sanders' voice carried across the café, and Quin spun around, seeming to shrink.

"I told you not to get them involved," Quin hissed at Kyle, though her voice didn't have its normal confidence.

"You didn't tell me that she was your teacher," Kyle retorted.

Before Quin could respond, Mrs. Sanders had reached them. "Quin, can I have a word with you?"

"I was just—"

"In my office."

Confusion flicked across Quin's face, then a slight smirk replaced it. Without another word, she followed Mrs. Sanders out of the café.

Kyle was about to follow, when Paul's voice came from the doorway.

"Kyle, Ocean. Come here, right now."

Kyle had never heard him so stern before. Slowly, he and Ocean walked over to Paul, who grabbed their hands and pulled them deeper into the hallway. Suddenly, a door opened to their right.

"All clear. You guys can come in," Mrs. Sanders said, popping her head out.

His mind reeling, Kyle followed Paul into what appeared to be the kitchen, Ocean right behind him. As soon as they were all inside, Mrs. Sanders closed the door. She turned to face the three of them, smiling.

"Everyone, meet my former student, Quin Smith."

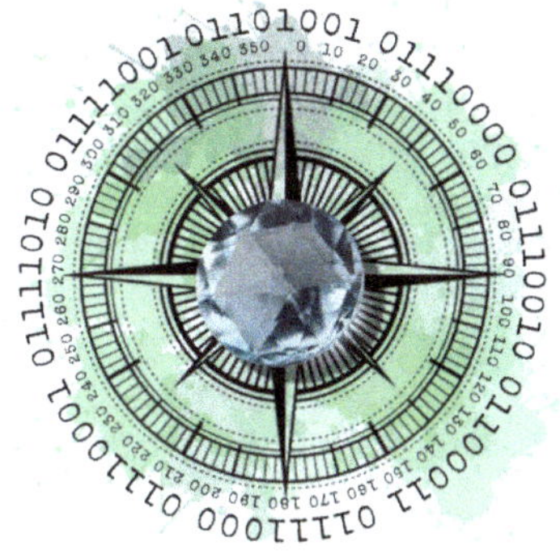

"So, let me get this straight." Ocean sat down on one of the metal tables, staring Quin down. "You wrote the note to warn us that there was a murderer after the necklace—the same necklace Kyle's mother wore when *she* died. Am I missing anything?"

"Not unless you count the fact that I'm a secret agent and that I'm going to get you off this boat." Quin smirked, though no one else smiled. "But right now, there's an even bigger problem."

"You mean bigger than an assassin chasing us down?" Mrs. Sanders asked, incredulous.

"Yes. Apparently, there are some pretty hungry people out there and we're the only ones in the kitchen." She winked, and Kyle caught the hint of a smile on Mrs. Sanders' lips. "And if anyone asks," Quin continued, "you all are on a behind-the-scenes tour and I'm showing you how the kitchen works." She grinned, slipping on an apron. "Come on. We have five orders to fill and we're down a barista."

"I guess I forgot to mention that she would make you work," Kyle whispered to Ocean, taking an apron off the wall and slipping it on.

"I thought we were supposed to be *having* breakfast, not making it," Ocean grumbled, tentatively brushing her hair back with her hands and tying on an apron.

Mrs. Sanders reluctantly put on a pair of gloves, walking past a long metal counter to a huge black fridge. "So we just wait until tomorrow when the ship docks and get off."

"No," Quin said, slicing a piece of orange. "That's what they expect. If we play their game, they'll win."

"Quin!" Mrs. Sanders spun around, her calm expression gone. "This isn't a game! And your family isn't the one in danger!"

"That's why I won't let you walk into a trap," Quin shot back, emphasizing her words with a loud thwack.

"So what's *your* plan, then?"

Quin pursed her lips. "I...can't tell you."

"So you want us to blindly trust you? You're not even an adult."

Quin flinched like she had been slapped. "Just because I'm not eighteen doesn't mean I can't think for myself."

"Stop it!" Ocean suddenly shouted, and Mrs. Sanders and Quin both turned to her. "None of this is helping. You said we don't have much time. Arguing isn't going to help anything."

Mrs. Sanders took a deep breath. "You're right. So what do we do?"

"I think the first thing to do," Paul said, stepping out of the corner, "is to figure out *who* is after you."

Kyle had completely forgotten about Paul, and judging by the others' startled looks, they had too. How *did* he manage to slip into the shadows so easily?

"It would have to be someone who has some sort of access to you. If they're a good agent, he or she would either get close to you or stay far away," Quin said, scraping the fruit into a bowl. "Is there anyone who seems suspicious?"

"There's the lifeguard," Kyle offered. "She seems like she might be suspicious."

Mrs. Sanders shook her head. "This isn't going to get us anywhere. I'm sure we've met at least twenty people on the cruise, and any one of them could be the agent." She turned back a pail of dough on the counter.

"You're right." Quin pursed her lips, obviously struggling with an idea. "So we have to narrow it down."

"Quin." Mrs. Sanders' voice held a warning. "What are you planning?"

Quin stopped chopping. "We have to figure out who is after you, and there's only one place you can go to get enough information for that."

For a moment, Mrs. Sanders' puzzled expression matched everyone else's, then she seemed to realize what Quin was saying. Her eyes went wide. "Quin! That's ridiculous! We can't just—"

"Break into the security room?" Quin finished, ginning. "You're right. It must be *way* harder than breaking into a top secret facility stocked with trained assassins."

Kyle watched in confusion as Mrs. Sanders' face flushed a bit. *Top secret facility?* She was sounding more and more like a spy every hour.

"That was Jill," Mrs. Sanders whispered.

"But you still followed her. Plus, you have me."

"And me," Paul said, making Mrs. Sanders jump.

Kyle grinned. Now she knew how he felt every time she snuck up on him.

"I'm pretty good at stealth." Paul winked at Kyle. "I'd say it's our best bet with so little time, and with two secret agents it should be a piece of cake."

"Speaking of cake," added Quin, "we need to get those bagels boiling and the bread baking. And then maybe I'll go 'wake up' the other barista so I can have a break."

Mrs. Sanders' eyes widened, and Quin smirked.

"Okay, so maybe it's more food poisoning than a virus. He should be feeling better by now."

"You poisoned him?! Quin, that's..." Mrs. Sanders paused, pursing her lips. "...Just like you."

"How was I supposed to know the difference between cherries and chokecherries?" Quin winked.

"All right, so what's the plan?" Paul asked, interrupting yet another argument.

"Well that's simple," Quin said, turning to him. "We just walk through the door."

THE HALLWAY WAS QUIET and empty as Kyle and Mrs. Sanders made their way toward the security room. Unlike last time, however, Kyle felt like his legs were made of jelly. If this was what being a spy was like, he wasn't so sure he wanted to be one.

Mrs. Sanders suddenly stopped, and he shook himself out of his thoughts. They had reached the glass door. She took a deep breath, then opened the door and stepped inside the simple reception room, with him right behind her.

The man behind the large oak desk looked up distractedly. "How can I help you?"

Mrs. Sanders cleared her throat. "We wanted to check in to see how the investigation is going." When the guard only gave her a blank stare, she continued, "It's about the note I found."

"Right. Of course." He smiled at her, standing up. "Please take a seat." He was so focused on Mrs. Sanders that he didn't even notice as Kyle slipped around the desk.

The back of the desk was open, with empty soda cans spilling out of a trash can and full ones stacked in little shelves along the bottom. Apparently this guard didn't have anything better to do than drink soda all day. Quickly, Kyle scanned the desk for the intercom. There, just where Quin had said it would be, was the white slanted box. His heart pounding, he followed the cord to a huge outlet strip. He tried not to think that at any moment, the guard could spot him. Hands shaking, he pulled the plug. Immediately, there was a click and the computer screen went black. *Great.* Of course he had pulled the wrong cord.

"Not again…" The guard sighed as Kyle reemerged beside Mrs. Sanders. He pressed a few keys on the keyboard, then sighed again. "Hold on. I'll be right back."

With that, he walked over to a door behind the desk, punching in a series of numbers Kyle couldn't keep track of. Hopefully, Mrs. Sanders could. He couldn't believe their plan had actually worked despite his mistake.

As soon as the guard was gone, Mrs. Sanders touched her ear. "Foxtrot, Alpha, Charlie, Alpha, Delta, Echo."

A minute later, the man came back, with another skinnier guard beside him. The second guy ducked under the desk. After a moment, there was a click and he stood up, shaking his head. "Got unplugged again. You really need to watch your feet. And empty your trash." He gave the big guard a pointed look, then turned away and headed back through the door.

Suddenly the glass door behind Kyle opened, and he turned to see Ocean, her eyes red and puffy as if she had been crying. She looked around the room, her eyes wide.

"Hey," the guard said, stepping out from behind the desk, his voice soft and gentle. Ocean had a way of doing that to people, which was why she had been chosen to be the lost child.

"Hey," the guard repeated. "It's going to be okay. What happened?"

"My—my dad. I can't find him. I looked everywhere..." Tears welled up in her eyes, and Kyle found himself almost believing her.

"It's okay. We're going to find him." The guard glanced down at her prosthetic leg, and for a moment, he looked a little shocked.

Heat built up inside Kyle, but then he remembered how he had stared at her the first time he had seen her.

Apparently, Ocean was used to it, or she was just really good at acting, because she didn't seem to notice. "W-we were in the garden and I stopped to look at a flower. When I looked up" —she paused to take a shaky breath— "he wasn't there." She started crying, her tears falling to the tiled floor, and Kyle couldn't help feeling sorry for her, even though he knew it was just an act.

"All right. We're going to find your father." The guard turned toward Mrs. Sanders and Kyle. "I'm just going to be a minute." With that, he headed for a door to their right. As he opened it, Kyle could see a brightly colored carpet, short shelves of toys, and cartoonish animals painted on the walls.

The guard disappeared into the room with Ocean, and without hesitating, Mrs. Sanders reached up to her ear.

"The milk's in the fridge. Could you get it for me?"

Kyle waited for a few agonizing seconds. The guard could come back any second and then the whole plan would fall apart.

"I prefer orange juice."

Kyle jumped, spinning around to see Quin standing just inches from him and Mrs. Sanders, rolling her eyes.

"Just get it," Mrs. Sanders sighed, walking over to the door and punching in the code.

Kyle backed up as Quin pressed herself against the wall and nodded, her face set. Mrs. Sanders pressed enter and pushed the door open. Without a moment's hesitation, Quin rushed through. The sound of electricity spilled out of the open door, and Kyle saw the skinny guard fall onto the floor, unconscious.

"All clear," Quin called, reappearing at the door. "These guards decided to take a short nap, but we have to be quick."

Swallowing, Kyle entered the carpeted room, closing the door behind him. On one wall hung at least ten monitors, each switching between different views of the ship. Against the other wall were three huge filing cabinets, which Quin was already rummaging through, peeking at every file.

"What do you want me to do?" Kyle asked, glancing uneasily at the unconscious guards.

"Just watch the security monitors," she said without looking up.

Trying to ignore the men on the floor, he turned to the monitors. He found himself being drawn in by the videos of people just doing normal things. One family was laughing in the café, then a baby in a high chair dropped something that burst open on the floor, spilling what was probably milk. The family stopped laughing and turned to the barista, a man with a short beard, who was walking up to them.

Kyle suddenly understood why someone would want to be a security monitor. They got to sit in a chair and see hundreds of people just going about life, unaware they were being watched or just not caring.

Something in the far right monitor caught his eye, and he turned to see one of the videos go black. A second later, the view of a maroon hallway filled the screen again. It almost seemed familiar. He walked over to get a better look.

It was a shot of a cabin hallway. He caught his breath when he saw the number on one of the doors. *71*. It was his cabin!

The picture suddenly changed to a view of another hallway, where a brown-haired lady was hurrying along. As she stepped out of the shot, another video came up with the same lady. The cameras were tracking her. As she got closer to the camera, she put her head down, as if studying the floor. *Or avoiding the camera.* The camera switched again, this time back to the shot of his cabin. The lady was gone. He waited for a few seconds, the only sound coming from Quin rummaging through the cabinet. Still the view didn't change. Then, so fast he almost missed it, their door swung closed. He did a double-take, turning to Quin, then back to the feed. He was sure it hadn't been open. Plus, if both he and Mrs. Sanders were here, who was in their room? *Maybe it's just the cleaning lady.*

Suddenly, a quiet beep came from the door, followed by five more. A movement in the bottom left screen caught his eye and his heart skipped a beat. Four security guards were right outside the door. Mrs. Sanders was talking with them, but they didn't seem to be stopping. He heard the click of the door just as he saw one of the guards barge into the room.

"Hands in the air where I can see them!"

Kyle's head snapped up to see the guards spilling into the room, guns pointed at him and Quin. He found he couldn't move, couldn't even breathe. He tried to wrap his mind around what was happening, but he couldn't.

"I said hands in the air!"

One of the guards rushed forward and grabbed Kyle, spinning him around while another one seized Quin.

"You're under arrest for breaking and entering, assaulting two officers, and accessing private information," the officer holding Quin said. "I would read you your rights" —something metal clicked as Quin was probably handcuffed— "but on this ship you don't have any."

The guard behind Kyle pushed him forward, forcing him to walk.

Kyle couldn't believe it. They couldn't have gotten caught. There had to be some way out of this. He looked at Quin for help, but her head was down, her arms bent awkwardly behind her with the handcuffs on her wrists. The guards must have thought she was more of a threat than he was.

As they emerged into the security waiting room, he caught sight of Mrs. Sanders, also in handcuffs. She looked straight at him, giving him a reassuring nod. Then they were hauled out the glass door and into the hallway, heading for the elevators. It took him a few seconds to realize that Quin wasn't with them.

"Where are we going?" Kyle asked, expecting the guard to tell him to shut up.

"To your cabin," the man replied instead. "You'll be under house arrest for the remainder of this trip. I hope you realize how serious what you did was."

Kyle just nodded, tears welling up in his eyes.

The man behind him sighed. "The captain will hear about this and he's a pretty merciful guy. He'll probably let you off at Marathon."

But we're not going to last until we get to Marathon. The thought made his heart race. This would be the perfect time for whoever was after them to strike.

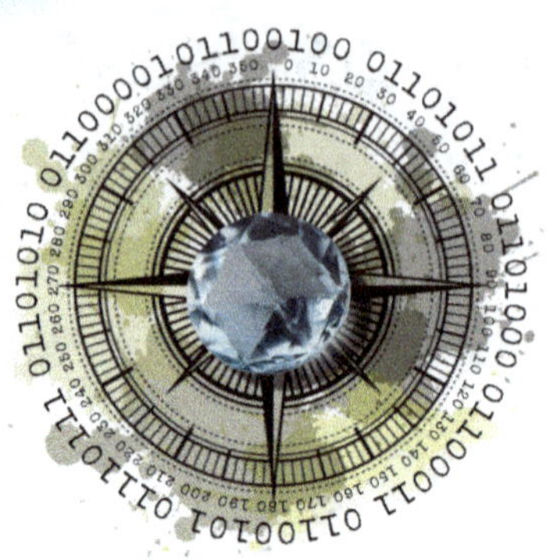

23

A KNOCK SOUNDED, AND Kyle's heart jumped. No one was supposed to be visiting them while they were under "cabin arrest." He glanced at Mrs. Sanders, who was sitting on her bed. She gave him a cautious look, then slowly got up and walked over to the door. The knock came again, and she grabbed her purse before opening the door.

"Mrs. Sanders?" the guard standing there asked, looking up from her clipboard.

"Yes," Mrs. Sanders replied simply. "Can I help you?"

"I'd like to ask you a few questions. If you'll please come with me..." The lady stared at Mrs. Sanders impatiently.

"I'm sorry. I can't leave Kyle."

"If you're worried about the note, we found the person who wrote it and she said it was just a joke. Don't worry," the woman added when Mrs. Sanders glanced at Kyle. "He'll be guarded. No one can get in or out."

Mrs. Sanders sighed, turning to Kyle.

"I'll be fine," Kyle found himself saying, though inside, his heart was racing. They both knew that the agent after them wouldn't let a few guards get in the way.

"All right. Make it quick."

The lady nodded, then turned and headed away without even checking to make sure Mrs. Sanders was following. Mrs. Sanders gave Kyle one last worried glance before going out, closing the door behind her. Kyle was alone.

Sighing, he walked over to the window, staring out at the horizon. Maybe he would die of boredom before the agent got to him. If they were going to put him under house arrest, they should have at least given him something to do other than play board games by himself.

He couldn't get the image of Beth walking down the corridor out of his mind. What *had* she been doing here? She hadn't taken the necklace. He'd been wearing it the whole time. Plus, she had only tried to help him. *So why was she here?* Something about it just seemed off.

A knock startled him. Cautiously, he walked across the room to the door. Opening it a crack, he peered into the hallway to see Ocean standing there, twirling her hair. As soon as he had opened the door, she slipped in, closing it behind her.

"How did you—" Kyle started, but she cut him off.

"There weren't any guards there. One of them passed me in the hallway. But that's not important. I heard over one of their radios that we're going to dock in an hour." She started playing with her hair again. "Kyle, I have a bad feeling. Something's going to happen."

"Where's your dad?" Kyle asked, trying to change the subject.

Ocean frowned. "That's another odd thing. A guard came to our cabin and took him away for questioning. I'm sure I've seen her before..." She trailed off, scrunching her eyebrows together. She shook her head. "You still have the necklace?"

"Yeah, I've been wearing it this whole time, and the necklace you gave me is still in my mother's box."

"You sure the SD card's still in there?"

Kyle's stomach did a somersault. Why hadn't he checked that earlier? He pulled the necklace out from under his shirt, hesitated a second, then pulled the two halves of the dolphin apart. It was empty. The SD card was gone.

"Hold on. I just remembered she couldn't have taken the card."

Kyle looked at Ocean, confused. "What do you mean?"

"She couldn't have taken it because my dad has it. He's been running that program on it for the past day. It's still in his computer. Come on!" She hurried over to the door, and Kyle followed her out into the hallway, still holding the necklace. There was no way he was leaving it again.

The two of them rushed through the corridor, and Kyle found himself glancing around every few seconds to make sure there weren't any guards following. What would happen once they knew he was gone? Why had they left in the first place? He shook his head as he and Ocean entered the elevator and started up. She was right. Something felt wrong about all of this.

The elevator stopped, jolting him out of his thoughts, and together he and Ocean made a break for her cabin. Only once they were inside with the door closed did he relax, pressing his back to the wall and sliding to the floor. Ocean ran over to the desk near the window, fiddling with Paul's laptop.

"It's still here," she breathed, holding up the tiny chip. "How could something so small lead to something so... big?" She shook her head, tossing the card to Kyle.

For a second, his heart skipped a beat, but the card just dropped harmlessly to the carpet. Carefully, he picked it up and slid it into the slot in the necklace.

"So...now what?" Ocean asked, leaning against the desk. "Quin's under custody, my dad and your mom are being ques-tioned..." She trailed off, a pained look on her face.

"Unless they're not," Kyle said, reading her face.

"What if the agent has them? What if she wasn't a guard? I'm sure a secret agent could disguise herself as a guard. I should have stopped them. Now everyone who can help us is gone."

"Maybe not everyone. Come on." He stood up and turned back to the door.

"Wait. Where are we going?"

"To the café." The thought of leaving the safety of the room made him want to curl in a ball and stay here until the agent came for him, but he couldn't just give up.

"Quin's not going to be there. They're holding her in a cell until we dock."

Kyle turned to her. "Quin's not the only one trying to help. If we're going to figure out what Beth was up to, we're going to have to ask her."

Ocean's eyes widened, and for a moment, hot anger rushed through him. It wasn't fair that she didn't like Beth. She'd never given her a chance.

"All right."

Kyle blinked. "Really?"

"It's better than staying here and waiting to be kidnapped." Pushing past him, Ocean opened the door, and headed out into the hallway. When no one jumped out to grab her, Kyle followed.

"WELL, LOOKS LIKE YOUR friend's not here," Ocean said as they neared the café. The normally bright and cheery entrance was now dark, with a gold rope strung across the opening. A sign dangled from the center, reading, "We're sorry for the inconvenience. The café is currently closed. Please check back soon!"

Great. Where else could they find Beth? "Now what?" Kyle said aloud.

"Where else would she go? She must come here for a reason." Ocean closed her eyes, her forehead furrowing.

"Maybe she likes—"

"Coffee," Ocean interrupted, opening her eyes. "That's what's different about the café. It's not usually quiet, and it's bright..." Her eyes lit up. "I think I know where to find her. Come on."

She spun around and headed back the way they had come. Kyle followed her past the elevators, and toward the glass doors that opened out onto the deck. He almost rammed into her before he realized she had stopped dead, her body suddenly stiff.

"Ocean? Are you—"

"Oh, hey," a sickeningly familiar voice taunted. "Fancy meeting you two here."

There, just to their right, standing by the edge of the Amber Pool, was Brianna. Haley was nowhere to be seen.

"The question is, what are *you* doing here?" Brianna cocked her head, a smug grin on her face. "You know, Ocean, for someone who's afraid of the water, you tend to spend a lot of time around it." She took a step toward them, and Ocean reflexively moved backwards.

"Let me guess. You're not truly afraid of the water, are you? Not enough to stay away from it."

"Stop it!" Kyle yelled, though he found himself wanting to back away as she stepped toward him. *No.* He couldn't show fear.

"This isn't your battle, Kyle," she retorted. "Just lay off."

Kyle stood firm, despite his heart pounding in his ears. For all he knew, she could be the one trying to get the necklace, and here she was, a few feet away from it. "Brianna, stop! You don't get it. Ocean can't swim anymore. Why are you doing this?"

Brianna's eyes bored into him as he stepped closer. "You think that because you've been friends with Ocean for a few days that you know everything about her. Ocean and I were friends for *years* until she left."

"Because you pushed her away and bullied her!" Kyle took a step forward. Unfortunately, so did Brianna, so that they were now only a few feet apart. Now he couldn't back down.

"Did Haley tell you that? I bet she told you that I pushed her into the pool, that *I* abandoned *her*."

Kyle blinked, caught off guard for a second. "But you—"

"There's something you should know, Kyle." Brianna took another step forward so that she was right in his face. "You can't trust everyone, because everyone has their own side of the story." Finally, she moved away from him, turning to face Ocean. "But we both know the truth, don't we, Ocean? You're not afraid of the water. You're afraid of drowning like your mother and that fear has crippled you more than your leg."

Kyle turned to Ocean, who was now staring at Brianna, her eyes wide. He wanted to yell again at Brianna to stop, but his head was spinning. What if Haley had been lying? Who could he trust? He shook his head. Why should he trust Brianna? She had tried to kill both of them. Trust had gotten his mother killed.

"If you say you can't trust anyone, why should I trust you?" He took a step forward, and Ocean looked up at him, a flame in her eyes. Her voice, though, was quiet.

"No." She turned back to Brianna, looking her in the face. "I'm not afraid of you." Her voice trembled, but she continued, "And you're wrong."

She took a deep breath, and Kyle tensed. He knew what she was about to do, but something inside him wouldn't let him stop her. Slowly, she pulled the strap off her prosthetic and slid it off, then, squeezing her eyes shut, she launched herself off the rim of the pool and headfirst into the water. Kyle's heart froze. He watched her as she floated down toward the bottom. He waited for her to move. Still she didn't break the surface. Hesitating only a moment, he ran toward the water, but Brianna grabbed him. He struggled against her grasp, but she held him firmly.

"Just wait."

Panicking, he scanned the pool, watching Ocean floating along the bottom. He couldn't tell if she was swimming or unconscious. Twisting, he broke free of Brianna's grasp and without hesitating dove into the water. The cold momentarily shocked him as he started swimming downwards, pulling against the drag of his clothes. She couldn't drown. A vision of his mother falling into the ocean flashed through his mind. Opening his eyes, he saw Ocean a few feet away, kicking with one leg and pulling herself up to the surface. Quickly, he swam upwards, relief flooding him.

As soon as he surfaced, he swam her way, blinking the water from his eyes. She whipped around as he came near, and he could see the fear on her face as she struggled to stay afloat. Before he could reach her, she dove underwater, swimming  away from him awkwardly. She surfaced further down, gasping in air.

"As long as you don't believe you can swim, you won't be able to." Brianna's voice carried across the water.

"Ocean, stop!" Kyle found himself shouting. "You're going to drown!" Even saying the words drove a spike of pain through him. She couldn't drown. Not like his mother.

Ocean sank beneath the surface, and Kyle dove, swimming toward her. Suddenly, something raced past him, and he spun around, scanning the water for Ocean. *There!* A blurry figure darted down. *Ocean?* It couldn't be. He surfaced, scanning the pool. Suddenly, the water exploded next to him, and for a moment, he saw a streak of blonde hair, then Ocean disappeared below the surface. He almost couldn't believe it. The girl who had just been struggling to stay afloat was racing through the water. She popped up beside him, her hair clinging to her head as she grinned, then just as quickly she dove back down.

Suddenly, something slammed into him, and he was knocked underwater. He tried to swim away, but whatever or whoever had rammed him had pinned his arms to his sides. He opened his eyes, but all he could make out was a blurry red blob. *Brianna?*

His head burst into the air, and he took a deep breath, blinking. Then, he looked around, and his heart rose into his throat. All around him was water. His head was in some sort of bubble. Another head broke into the small space, and Kyle blinked. *Quin?*

"Sorry it's so small. I had to make it out of a salad bowl and a bunch of rolling pins." Her voice sounded tinny.

"How—why are you here?" he asked, his heart still pounding as he tried to get used to breathing with the surface so high above him.

"It's complicated. But we only have about thirty seconds before people start wondering what's happening and we run out of air. Kyle, the ship's going to dock in about half an hour. Something's wrong. If there is an agent after you, which we know there is, he or she should have gone after the necklace a long time ago. Where's your mom? I need to talk to her."

Kyle blinked, already finding it harder to breathe. "A lady took her away for questioning." The look on Quin's face made him stop.

"When did she take her?" The urgency in her voice made his heart jump.

"About ten minutes ago. Why?"

"I jammed their radio signals fifteen minutes ago. Plus, there aren't any female guards on the ship. What if the agent isn't after the necklace? What if she's after your mom?"

24

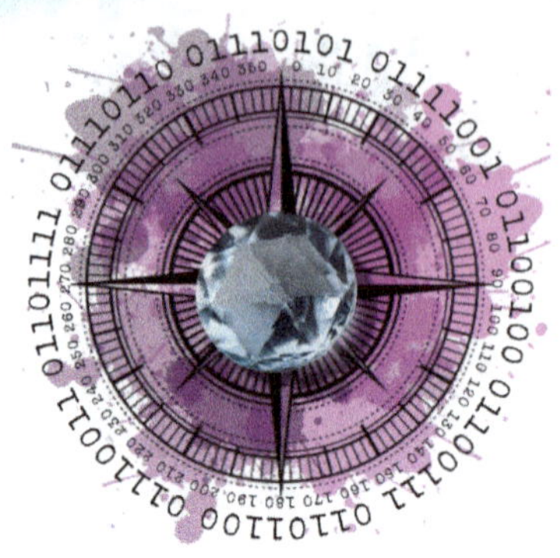

"So, what do we do now?" Ocean asked as they hurried down the hallway, leaving wet footprints on the carpet.

"We're going to have to figure out where the agent is keeping them," Quin replied.

But what if the agent has already...No. He couldn't think like that. Mrs. Sanders had escaped before. She couldn't have been caught.

"And how—"

"Please, just be quiet. I need to think." Quin took a deep breath, then stopped, turning to face them. "I'm sorry. This must be hard for you. But right now, we have to be cautious. So no more talking." She spun back around and started walking again.

"How did you get out, anyway?" Ocean asked.

"It's a long story. And right now, we don't have time. We know that there's an agent on the boat, and that the agent probably has your parents. We know that the necklace has incriminating evidence, which is probably why the agent is here. We know that the person who took Kyle's mom away wasn't a guard, since she was a female. What we need to find out is who the agent is and who took your parents."

"We have to find them," Ocean said, panicking. "The lady who took my dad looked like Elizabeth Quigley."

Quin nodded.

"Wait, you knew?" Kyle asked, incredulous.

"I'm sorry, but I didn't want to tip her off." Quin glanced at Kyle. "Though she probably already knows I know, which is why we need to act fast."

"If we know who took our parents, why don't we find her and get them back instead of just talking?!" Ocean shouted, turning and storming away.

"Ocean, wait!" Quin called out. "Just because we probably know who took them, doesn't mean we can just march up to her. We need a plan."

Ocean spun to face her. "All we ever do is plan! We need to *do* something!"

"I know, but we can't play Beth's game. If we do, she'll win. We need to do something she doesn't expect."

"Then what's your plan?" Ocean asked.

"Even if she's after your parents, we still have something she wants. The necklace."

"So?" Kyle asked, glancing from Quin to Ocean.

"So, we use the necklace to bargain for your parents."

"You can't just hand over the necklace. That's what she wants us to do. You said it yourself; we can't play by her rules."

"So, how are we supposed to find her exactly?" Ocean interrupted, scanning the top deck from the safety of the little walkway between two restaurants. For some reason, whoever had designed the ship had left a gap between those buildings, forming a sort of alley. Kyle still had no idea why Quin had decided to come here of all places.

"And how do you know Beth will have our parents?" Kyle objected, fingering his necklace. Something was off about this whole thing. How did Quin know what Beth was planning? How had she escaped? Nothing added up.

You want your mom back, then you have to sacrifice the necklace.

When Quin had first said he'd have to let the necklace go, it had seemed like the only way. Now, he wasn't so sure if he could. It was the last thing that connected him to his parents. Why had Mrs. Sanders given it to him in the first place?! None of this would have happened if she hadn't.

"Kyle, you have to trust me."

"Why should we trust you when you're obviously hiding something?" Kyle turned on Quin, who glanced at Ocean.

"You know that as long as you have the necklace, the Rose is going to chase you and Mrs. Sanders." Quin spun back to face him. "What would you rather have, the necklace or your life?"

Before he could respond, she yanked the necklace off him, breaking the chain. He barely noticed the sting in his neck as he stared at her.

"You broke it!" He grabbed for the necklace, but she turned away, touching her ear.

"I have the necklace. Now give their parents back."

It took a few seconds for him to realize what was happening. "No!" he shouted, launching himself at Quin, who easily stepped aside.

"Nicely done, Quin," said a familiar voice from behind them. Kyle spun around to see Beth emerge from around one of the buildings. "Honestly, you don't seem like the betraying type."

"Where are they?" Quin snapped, staring Beth down like she might bite her head off.

"You'll see them when I have the necklace." Beth coyly walked up to Quin, which only seemed to make Quin more angry.

"How could you!" Kyle couldn't help the anger that surged through him as he glared at Beth. "I thought you were trying to help us!"

"You trusted me," Beth said simply. "You of all people should know you can't trust anyone."

"What you do is wrong!" Quin hissed. "I don't understand how someone can be so evil."

"Evil? What I don't understand is how someone could send children out into the field to be killed!"

"I'm not a child! It just so happens people don't think I'm an adult. In other countries I would already be married."

"You know what's wrong with sending children to do adult work?" Beth continued as if she hadn't heard Quin. "Children are inexperienced, untrained, and naive."

"You're twisted!" Quin snarled. "How could you actually think what you're doing is right? You're the one trying to kill us!"

"Right is arbitrary. It's a way to make yourself feel better about doing something. What we do is good. Good for the people, good for us—"

"And good for your wallets."

Beth narrowed her eyes, her face turning red. "I don't expect *you* to believe me. But I do expect you to hand over the necklace."

"Fine. Is this what you wanted?" Quin tossed the necklace to Beth. For a moment, it hung in the air, and Kyle imagined it hitting the deck and shattering. Then it was in Beth's hand. *Honestly, it probably would have been better if it had shattered.*

"Actually, it isn't." Beth pulled something shiny out of her overshirt. Quin's face went white. It took a second for Kyle to recognize the object. Beth was holding a gun.

"So that was your mission all along? You were sent here to kill us?"

The remark sent a pang of fear through Kyle and he looked up at the two women. Out of the corner of his eye he could see Ocean edging backward, toward the railing.

"You're very perceptive." Beth grinned. "I wonder how your parents will feel when they realize they're the reason you died." As she spoke, she moved closer to them, pushing them backward toward the edge of the ship.

Without warning, Quin took a step forward, and Beth narrowed her eyes.

"Don't forget I'm the one with the gun," she said without a hint of fear.

"Maybe," Quin said, scanning the surroundings, "but with God, all things are possible. Through Jesus, we have no fear of death. Even though we're weak, God makes us strong."

"I don't care!" Beth hissed. "Let's see if your God can save you now. You have two options. Either you jump off the side of the ship, or I'll pull the trigger and you all die anyway." She edged closer to the railing behind them and Quin took a step back. "Personally, I like the first option better. It makes for a better cover story." She slipped her finger onto the trigger of the gun.

Kyle's heart was pounding so fast it made it hard to think clearly.

Ocean's eyes were wide, and she looked like she was about to faint.

No one moved.

"All right, I'll give you five seconds to decide. Five—"

Kyle glanced down at the foaming water far below, suddenly feeling nauseous in the bright daylight.

"—four—"

Quin crouched in a defensive position, and Ocean looked away.

"—three, two—"

Beth flicked a switch on the gun, aiming it at Kyle.

"One."

The next moment went by in a flash. Quin leaped backward, and Kyle felt her arm smack into him, knocking him off balance. The world spun as his stomach lurched. All his muscles tensed, and he felt wind whipping around him. "Point your legs and feet down and put your arms by your sides!" Quin screamed through the roaring wind. The next moment a thunderous sound engulfed him and the world exploded into pain.

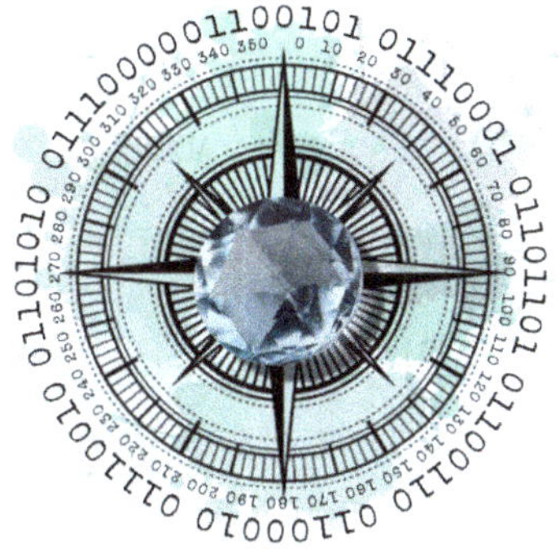

25

KYLE'S EYES FLEW OPEN, but this time what he felt wasn't a nightmare. It was real. Kicking off his shoes, he desperately swam upward, realizing he had no air in his lungs. His body stung like he'd fallen off a three story building. He couldn't tell how far away the surface was, or even if he was moving. No matter how hard he kicked, he didn't seem to be moving. He closed his eyes, using all his strength to keep swimming.

Something grabbed his arm and suddenly he was rising. His lungs now burned along with the rest of his body. A few seconds later, he broke the surface and started coughing, gasping in the fresh air. The person let go of his arm, and he plunged beneath the water again before swimming back to the surface. He was alive.

Ocean!

He opened his eyes just as another wave crashed over him. He came up coughing, scanning the water for her. But the only things he could see were the waves and the huge white side of the cruise ship slowly moving further and further away. *No.* He couldn't be overboard. His brain refused to believe it.

"Ocean!" he shouted, panic starting to flood him. Something bumped his leg, and his heart leapt. Quin's head broke through the surface right beside him, and she gasped, pulling Ocean's head up a moment later, her eyes closed. His body flooded with relief as she started coughing out water and gasping in air.

"Ocean, we're going to be fine. Just take some deep breaths." Quin's voice brought him back to the present, and he turned back to Ocean. Her face had gone pale and her eyes were squeezed shut. All he could do was watch as Quin tried to calm her. Everything had gone wrong. His mother's necklace was gone. They hadn't been able to thwart Beth's plan. Could he even trust Quin anymore? He had lost his mom, and now they were alone in the middle of the cold ocean.

Without warning, he turned to Quin, splashing her as anger boiled inside him. "You're the monster! You knew Beth wouldn't let us go! You knew you were leading us to her! You gave her the necklace!"

"Kyle, this isn't the time to fight! I'm trying to rescue you!" Quin scowled at him, which fueled his anger even more.

"You never cared about keeping us safe! Now we lost the necklace and our parents, and we're in the middle of the ocean, because of you!"

"Kyle!" Quin shouted, throwing water at him. "I do care about you! And we didn't lose the necklace." She reached down into the water with one hand, then pulled her hand back out, revealing a wooden dolphin hanging from a chain. Kyle snatched it from her, feeling around the tail of the dolphin. Right where the tail joined the body was a small uneven lump. His heart leapt in his chest.

"How?" he asked, still almost not believing it.

"I'll explain later."

Kyle splashed her again and she laughed.

"I told you I would find something to make you mad about." She playfully threw more water at him.

"But Beth almost killed us! How was that a good plan?!"

"I didn't see *you* come up with a better one!" Quin snapped, her calm expression changing to anger. "How was I supposed to know she had a gun?"

"Stop it!" Ocean shouted. Kyle turned to see her treading water beside Quin. "We're in the middle of the ocean—" A wave crashed over her, and she came up gasping. "Stop arguing!"

Before either of them could respond, Ocean's head slipped under the waves, again, and she gulped in air. Her eyes were closed, but he could tell she was trying not to panic. Quin quickly grabbed her, supporting Ocean's head and sending strong strokes through the waves.

"She's right. We need to focus on surviving." She took a deep breath. "Lord," she said quietly, "You've gotten me out of tricky situations before. Please, protect us now. Send us help. I know You're with us. Give us strength."

The simple words sent a pain through Kyle's chest. Quin spoke to God like He was right there above her. Like He was her father. Kyle remembered the last time he had felt that. The last time he had prayed. If God had been there, He wouldn't have let Kyle's parents die.

"Ocean?" Quin's voice called from his right, and he turned to see her frantically scanning the water. "Ocean!"

Kyle wiped his tears away, his heart suddenly pounding. Had Ocean slipped underwater? He had seen her swim in the pool, only surfacing for a second, then diving. *There!* Ocean's blonde hair popped out of the water, and she took a deep breath before submerging again. He started swimming toward her, battling the waves, trying to get a glimpse of her. When he didn't see anything, he took a deep breath and dove, the cold slapping him in the face.

His eyes stung as he forced them open, but all he saw was dark blue. Suddenly, a high-pitched whistle pierced the water. He spun around, trying to figure out where it was coming from, but it seemed to be all around him. There was another whistle, this one sounding a lot more like a dolphin's. Ignoring the urge to surface, he swam toward where he thought he had heard it, then he stopped as another whistle sounded behind him. He spun around, but all he could see was dark blue. Lungs begging for air, he swam up, gasping as he broke the surface.

Blinking the water out of his eyes, he looked around, relief flooding him as he saw Ocean's head a few yards away. He started swimming toward her, then froze. Her hands were wrapped around something gray and curved. His heart skipped a beat as he recognized the shape he had seen hundreds of times before. Ocean was holding onto a dolphin's fin. Kyle jerked as a puff of air exploded from his right and another fin broke the surface before disappearing. His breath lodged in his throat, from both awe and fear. Slowly, the huge mammal circled him, and he felt his legs buzz. He started at the feeling, and the dolphin shot away, returning a few seconds later and buzzing his legs again.

Finally, it seemed satisfied and slowly ascended, breaking the surface and letting out another blast of fishy air.

Kyle glanced over at Quin, who was staring at him, smirking. He turned back to the dolphin as it bumped up against him, letting out another high-pitched whistle. Slowly, he ran his hand along the dolphin's melon, avoiding the blowhole  like his mother had taught him. He looked up and blinked. It seemed so natural, even though it had been about four years since he had touched one.

"You know, we're not going to survive more than half an hour in the ocean. We have to get out of the water soon," Quin said, her voice beginning to shake with cold. "We were supposed to arrive at Marathon in about an hour. If the cruise ship was traveling 18 knots per hour, it means we're about 20 miles from land."

Kyle stared at her, his heart dropping as he realized what she meant.

"I'm sorry, Kyle. This is all my fault. I wanted to believe I could outsmart Beth and save you. She's right. I'm not experienced enough to be an agent. I wasn't even supposed to go on this mission." Quin whispered the last part.

"No, you're right," Ocean said, startling both of them. "You aren't good enough to be an agent, but God's more powerful than Beth. Who do you think sent the dolphins? He's with us. He'll protect us."

"I didn't know you..." Kyle trailed off.

"That I'm religious? You can just add that to the many different kinds of freaks I am." She grinned, and Kyle felt a little better.

Something bumped into him, and he saw a fin resting by his hand. Quickly, he swam away, his face burning as he felt Quin's eyes on him. The dolphin followed him, bumping its fin into him again.

"Stop it!" he hissed. He glanced up at Ocean, and suddenly realized what the dolphin was trying to do. It lifted its head out of the water, letting out a puff of air. For a moment, he gazed into its large blue eye. Kyle glanced at Quin, and he was surprised to see another dolphin rubbing up against her. She gave him an awkward smile. Taking a deep breath, he grabbed onto the fin, preparing himself for whatever was about to come, but the dolphin only nestled beneath him, raising him out of the water. He watched as another dolphin came up on the other side of Quin, offering its fin for her. She just stared at it, and Kyle grinned.

"It wants you to grab on!" he called out, and she glared at him but finally wrapped her hand around it. As if pulled by a string, all the dolphins started moving slowly, headed in the same direction. Ocean gripped her dolphin's fin for life as they started picking up speed, and Kyle suddenly realized she wasn't wearing her prosthetic. He reflexively looked away from her exposed stump, his face growing hot. In the side of his vision, he saw her look back at him, and a grin spread across her face. She wiggled her stump at him, and he wished the dolphin would dive underwater as his face burned.

"You think it's weird, don't you?" she called back to him. He didn't respond, and she continued. "Well, this is me. I'm a mutant. So now you can laugh. You can just turn away like everyone else. Like *you* did before."

"Ocean, it's not like that!" He blinked, falling silent. Had he really just said that? "We're friends. With or without one of us having a missing leg. I used to care about that, but I don't anymore."

Ocean turned away, hugging the dolphin she was riding on. Finally, she turned back to him, her eyes red. "I'm sorry. I just sometimes wondered why God gave me only one good leg. Brianna was the only other one who didn't care. But you saw what happened to her."

"Yeah. Maybe she was a bully, but she did help you overcome your fear."

Ocean looked ahead again. A spray of fishy air and water blasted Kyle, and he blinked, looking down through the water at the creature that had come to their rescue. Maybe Ocean was right. Maybe God had sent the dolphins. But if He had, why had He saved Kyle when He hadn't even tried to save his parents?

"Kyle, look!" Ocean shouted, and he turned to where she was pointing. At first, he couldn't see anything but endless waves, then something yellow appeared in the water, disappearing a second later, then reappearing. He strained his eyes as they approached it, trying to make out what it was. It seemed like there was a sail attached to it. *A sailboat!*

"Looks like our rides here!" Quin announced, grinning.

Kyle closed his eyes, hugging the rubbery skin of the dolphin under him. How had they known? When he raised his head again, the odd sailboat was in clear view, bouncing along the waves on two long, thin hulls. As they neared the boat, a man's voice suddenly echoed off the water.

"Ahoy there, dolphin riders! Hold on, we're coming abreast!"

The dolphin Kyle was riding on slowed as the sailboat slowly turned, heading toward his right. As the boat grew nearer, he could make out a low cabin with a glass windshield reflecting the sea. A wave slapped into him as the boat slowed down to a stop a few yards away.

"Daddy, look! The dolphins are saving people!" A little boy's voice carried over the water, and Kyle looked up to see a crowd standing at a railing on one of the hulls. A man in a blue shirt and white pants, holding a megaphone, pushed through the crowd.

"If you swim behind the boat, you'll find a ladder on the hull."

The dolphin under Kyle let out a whistle, then swam down, letting him slip into the freezing water. He took a few deep breaths, getting used to the cold, then turned around to see Ocean swimming next to her dolphin, holding onto its head.

"Kyle, Ocean, come on!" Quin called, already swimming toward the boat. Kyle didn't move as he watched Ocean stroking the dolphin. Slowly, he swam over to her, placing his hand on her shoulder, not knowing what to say.

"My dad's gone," she said, rubbing the dolphin's head. "Our parents are both gone." She turned to face him, tears in her eyes. "What about Beth? Dad's still on the ship with her. What if they've been kidnapped, or worse?" The dolphin suddenly sank below the water, and Kyle saw its fin break the surface a distance away.

"What if they aren't?" Kyle's teeth were already chattering. "Come on. We need to get out of the water." With that, he turned and followed Quin. Ocean dove beside him, surfacing a few feet away, and then diving again, moving through the water like a dolphin. With a last glance at the pod that had rescued them, he swam for the ladder, grabbing onto one of the rungs and pulling himself up. He had no idea how long they had been in the water, and his legs shook as he climbed. Finally, he pulled himself up onto the deck, letting himself collapse on the solid wood.

26

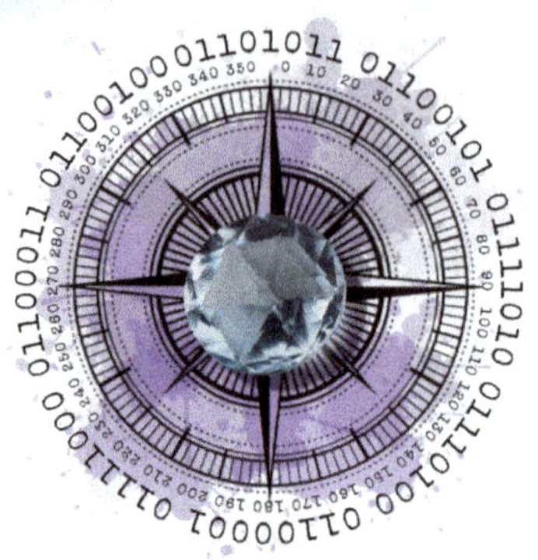

"How are you three doing?" the old weather-beaten captain asked, stepping into the ship's tiny dining room. "Warming up okay?"

"Yeah," Quin replied for them, unwrapping a towel from her hair. "Thank you."

Kyle glanced over at Ocean, who still had her head under the towel the captain, Keith, had given her, probably still crying. A lump grew in Kyle's throat as he thought of Ocean's father and Mrs. Sanders still on the cruise ship. Had they managed to fight off Beth? What if they were—no. They couldn't be dead. Not again.

"Hey, Kyle, Ocean, it's going to be okay. We'll find a way to get you and your parents back together," Quin said calmly, rubbing Ocean's back.

"It's going to be okay. God—"

"God doesn't care about us! Why would He save me when He killed my parents?" He glared at Quin, and for a moment, she just blinked, then she nodded.

"You're right," she said, looking him in the eyes. "If He killed your parents, why would we trust Him to help us? But He didn't kill your parents, Kyle. God gives us free will and with that, we're allowed to disobey Him, and one of His commands is to not murder. The agent who killed your parents knew what would happen."

Tears continued to burn his eyes, and his heart ached more than the cold in his limbs, but it was a good kind of pain, like when his father had to stick a needle in his finger to get a splinter out.

"And Kyle," she continued, "God cried when your parents died, even more than you, because He made them and knew everything about them. He loved them even more than you did."

It was like something broke inside him, and before he could stop it, he was crying. All he felt was the sharp pain and his tears burning down his cheek. Quin's hand rested on his shoulder, and what was left of the bottle holding his tears broke. "If God loved them, he wouldn't have let them die!"

Quin didn't respond for a second. "You believe in heaven, right?" she asked finally. When he nodded, she continued. "God's like a father. He wants to be with us forever, but He lives in heaven, and we live here, and as long as we're here we're separated from Him. Maybe God just wanted to be with them. But you know what? It doesn't matter how far away you are. Even though we're separated, He still hears us. You can pray to Him now," Quin said gently, "It doesn't matter how far away you feel. He's always right beside you. And since your parents are with Him, that means so are they."

Kyle took a deep shaky breath and closed his eyes. *God, I haven't talked to you for two years, but please help us now. I'm sorry I turned away from You. Jesus, help my mom. Don't let Beth kill them.* He opened his eyes, tears blurring his vision.

"There, that wasn't so hard." She sighed. "At least we're safe here," Quin noted, then she frowned. "But I still don't get why Beth just let us go. She must have known we would survive the fall."

"Maybe she thought no one would rescue us and we would freeze to—" Kyle cut himself off, wrapping his towel tighter over his damp shirt.

"That makes sense." Quin sighed. "I was kind of hoping maybe her heart wasn't completely hardened."

Kyle turned to the door as it opened and Keith stuck his head in. "We're about five minutes from land. Just wanted to let you know." Behind him, Kyle could see a strip of land lined with buildings in the distance.

"Where are we landing?" he asked.

Keith's wrinkled face lifted in a smile. "Marathon. Been my home for forty years."

Kyle glanced at Quin, but she didn't seem worried.

"Thanks again," she said. Keith nodded, then closed the door, heading back to the crowd on the deck.

"Isn't Marathon where the ship will dock?" Kyle asked.

"Yes." Quin smirked at him. "But we'll be gone before she even knows we landed."

Ocean's eyes grew wide as she seemed to realize what that meant. "No! We have to go back!" Tears welled up in her eyes again, and she buried her head in her towel.

"Ocean," Quin said gently, going back over to her and placing her hand on Ocean's shoulder, "it will all turn out fine. 'And we know that for those who love God all things work together for good, for those who are called according to his purpose'. No matter what happens, everything will turn out for good."

Kieth's head popped back in the door, grinning. "Ladies and gentle...man. We have officially docked. And there's someone to see you." He called back to a man behind him, and a few moments later, three men dressed in navy-blue uniforms entered the room, and Kyle's heart sped up. He had seen those uniforms before, two years ago. *No, please no.*

"Lieutenant Davis of the United States Coast Guard," one of the men said, offering a small smile. "This is Ensign Travis and Aviation Survival Technician Halfman." He grinned slyly. "We joke that he's half-man, half-fish." His grin faded as he took a seat across from them, the two other men following suit.

Kyle tried to block the memory, but it came anyway.

"Kyle Joseph Lawson?" the officer asked, glancing at a clipboard, then back at him. Kyle nodded. A reassuring hand gripped him, and he winced at his case worker's touch.

"We regret to inform you that your parents' bodies were found at 1 o'clock today. They were both found dead."

Just hearing those words sent a fresh searing pain through Kyle, and without warning, he sprinted from the table, leaving his chair to crash to the floor. NO! They weren't dead! Even though he had seen his mother fall into the ocean, he still couldn't believe it. Sobs escaped his chest, and he sank to the floor, his back to the wall. The pain inside was worse than anything he had ever felt. Even tearing his leg open falling off his bike hadn't hurt like this. God, I hate you! I hate *you!*

"Kyle," a voice said gently, ripping him out of his thoughts.

"I understand this is probably hard for you," the lieutenant continued when Kyle looked up at him. "What happened? Why were you out in the ocean? Did you fall off a ship?"

Kyle glanced at Ocean and Quin, and he realized with a start that they were now at separate tables, each being interviewed.

"Kyle, listen to me. We can help you find your parents. Just—"

Kyle shut his eyes, remembering images of the *Emerald Wind* broken on the rocks and his mother slipping off the deck into the ocean. The officer's words echoed through his head. *"They were both found dead."* They had already found his parents—dead. And now his mom was gone.

"Actually, you can't."

The lieutenant spun towards Quin, giving her a curious scowl. "What do you mean we can't? We—"

"They're gone."

Kyle felt his stomach flip. He tried to ask what she meant, but he couldn't get the words out.

"What do you mean?" the lieutenant snapped, reaching for his radio.

Silently, Quin reached into her ear, and Kyle almost gagged as she pulled out what looked like a ball of earwax.

"They've gone missing."

Kyle didn't hear the rest of what she said. Everything seemed to blur around him. "What do you mean they're missing?!" He knew he was yelling, but he couldn't stop himself. "I thought—"

"Kyle." Quin gripped his shoulders, forcing him to look at her face. "They're fine. Mrs. Sanders just said they'd escaped and were going undercover. We'll find them."

Kyle let out a breath as relief washed over him.

For a moment, the lieutenant stared at her, as if trying to wrap his mind around what she had just said, then he pressed the button on his radio. "Tylor, sir, this is Lieutenant Davis." He glanced at Kyle and the others. "Permission to bring the children on to the base. Over."

"Permission granted, lieutenant. Over and out," a husky voice on the radio responded.

"All right then." Standing up, Lieutenant Davis motioned to the door. "Let's get this all sorted out."

"Yes, ma'am," the base commander muttered into the phone, pacing the small tiled room they were in. "Yes, ma'am. I'm sure you do."

Kyle stared up at the way-too-bright light above them, annoyed at the one-way conversation.

"Yes, ma'am, but we'll need proof before we can release them."

Kyle glanced over at Quin, then quickly looked away, anger growing in him again, though not before she let out a sigh.

"Kyle, look, I'm sorry," she said for the fifth time. "But we *will* find them. It'll just take time."

"And why should we trust you?" he shot back, although he already knew what she was going to say. She had saved them and the necklace, but she had also almost gotten them killed.

"You shouldn't," Quin said, quietly.

He looked up at her, noticing for the first time that she was biting her lip. Okay, he hadn't been expecting *that*.

"I shouldn't have even gone on this mission. I convinced my parents it would be safe, but I knew it wouldn't. I'm sorry, Kyle. Maybe if an adult had gone—"

"We wouldn't have the necklace," Kyle couldn't help blurting out. Out of the corner of his eye, he saw two officers glance at each other, probably confused. "Mrs. Sanders would have just given the necklace to Beth and then got us off the ship, but you saved the necklace *and* got us off."

"Sorry to interrupt," the base captain cut in, "but we've gotten everything cleared up. You'll be leaving as soon as we get the helicopter ready."

"Thanks again," Quin said, smiling at him.

He tipped his hat at her. "Ma'am, it's our job to protect." With that, he headed out of the room.

"All right," the lieutenant said, standing up. "Let's get you guys suited up."

T HE WHIRRING OF THE helicopter's rotors thundered overhead as they headed for a small island barely off the main coast.

The pilot said something to AST Halfman that Kyle couldn't understand, and the officer nodded, speaking into his headset. Floating near the island was a large boat that looked almost like the *Emerald Wind.* Kyle swallowed, glancing at Ocean, who was staring out the window, not looking at Quin or him. Quin had tried to comfort her when they got in the helicopter, but Ocean had just glared at her, and he didn't blame her.

"We're coming up on Crystal Academy. We're going to land on the water about a hundred yards from the beach," a voice crackled above the noise of the engine. "Please stand by."

Kyle gripped his seat harder as the helicopter tilted forward, slowly descending toward the water. As they lowered, the helicopter slowed, and with a slight jolt, they touched down. Immediately, the helicopter started rocking, moving with the waves. One of the men got out of his seat and unstrapped a bright yellow rubber package from the wall, then opened the door and threw it into the waves. With a whoosh of air, it unfolded into a lifeboat.

The man turned to the three of them, motioning for them to get into it. Kyle watched Quin unbuckle and walk over to Ocean, though he couldn't hear what she said over the sound of the engine. The man motioned to Kyle again and he quickly unstrapped himself, wobbling as he tried to stand up. He hesitated as he stared out at the island. What would his life be like when he got to the academy? Would he ever see Mrs. Sanders again?

Taking a deep breath, he slowly walked over to the door. The man standing there lifted him and placed him in the raft. A few seconds later, Ocean and Quin joined him, and he could tell Ocean had been crying.

As soon as everyone was in the raft, the man stepped in, grabbing a fold-out paddle from the side. The roar of the engine slowly got quieter as they headed away from the bright orange helicopter and toward the shore of the island.

Just when he thought his life might stay the same, everything had flipped upside down again. He was now heading to an academy he hadn't even known existed until a few days ago.

God, why do You keep on changing everything? But maybe this was just the next step in his life. After all, Quin had said the Crystal would bring Mrs. Sanders and Paul back, and he had Ocean and Quin. Maybe everything was actually somehow better than when he had left on the cruise. At least Beth now thought they were dead, which meant she wouldn't be coming after them again. It seemed like so long ago that he had walked onto the ship for the first time.

Blinking out of his thoughts, Kyle gazed at the trees on the shoreline, and he thought he could just make out a brick building through them.

"There it is," Quin said, a sense of pride in her voice. She turned to them and grinned. "Kyle, Ocean, welcome to the academy."

Epilogue

KYLE LET OUT A breath into the cool sea air as he headed toward the figure sitting on the beach, her prosthetic lying next to her in the sand. Quin stood a few feet away, throwing stones into the waves. He couldn't hear what they were saying over the crashing waves, but it probably had something to do with Ocean's dad.

"Hi, Kyle." Quin smiled at him, as he sat down in the sand beside Ocean, who just stared down away from him.

For a moment, he sat there, looking out at the ocean where his mom had gone missing. As soon as he'd grown close to his mom, she'd gone, just like his other parents. *God, why? Why take away every parent I get?*

"It doesn't matter how far away you feel. He's always right beside you. And since your parents are with Him, that means so are they." That's what Quin had said.

"Where do you think they are?" Ocean's small voice came from next to him. It had been about two weeks since they had been forced to separate, and every day it was harder to imagine them coming back.

Kyle shook his head. "I don't know. Maybe they're in a seafood diner eating a huge red lobster." He let a small smile through. It was a sort of game they had started playing when they had first arrived at the academy. It made Mrs. Sanders and Paul seem closer to imagine them, even if it was doing ridiculous things like skydiving out of a plane or hiking a hundred miles to find them.

"You realize you two only smile when you're together?" Quin asked, smirking. "Are you sure you're not secretly siblings?"

Kyle grinned, and he could see Ocean's neck turn even more red than it already was.

"So, Kyle," Quin said, "how are you doing? Maybe I can at least get *something* out of one of you. How are summer classes for you?"

Kyle swallowed, looking down at the sand. At least they gave him something to do beside thinking about his mom, somewhere out there.

"Come on! I need something out of you. I can't see inside your brain!"

Kyle smirked. "I still don't remember what the study of fish is called, I haven't finished signing the alphabet, I can't quite swim half a mile yet, and I have no idea why I'm even doing all this!"

"Okay..." Quin held up her hands. "Forget I asked. What I meant to say was..." She suddenly trailed off, staring behind Kyle. "That's odd..."

He turned to see three people coming toward them, two wearing full suits and ties, even though it was the middle of summer. The only thing that fit in were the sunglasses. The other person was Mrs. Smith, the principal who also happened to be Quin's mother.

Kyle got to his feet as they approached, and his heart started pounding, though it subsided when he saw Mrs. Smith's smile.

"What are you doing here?" Quin asked her mom, glancing at the other two strangers. "And who are they?"

"Hi to you too, Quin." Her mother's thin lips smiled, then she turned to Kyle. "Kyle, Ocean, I want you two to meet Doctor..." She glanced at the clean-shaven man. "Ozvolve?" He nodded, and she continued. "And Heidi Snipe." She gestured to the woman who was busy biting her lip. "They've come a long way to see you two." She broke into a full smile that seemed to be hiding something and nodded to Heidi.

Kyle stared at Heidi. There was something familiar about her. He turned to look at Quin, but she only gave him an equally confused look. He turned to Ocean, but just as he caught sight of her, she ran into the man's arms, burying her head in his chest.

"Didn't fool you for a second." There was no mistaking it. It was Paul's voice.

Kyle spun toward the woman, his heart pounding again. Tears were now streaming down her face, and her sunglasses were on the sand, revealing his mom's face. He didn't know when he had run to her, or if he had, but he found himself engulfed in her arms. Suddenly, four more arms wrapped around them, as Ocean and Paul joined in.

"I'm so sorry, Kyle," his mom choked in his ear. "Every moment we were hiding, I wanted to go find you. You have no idea how many homes, churches, and homeless shelters we've been at." She paused for a moment. "I never stopped thinking about you. I'm so sorry."

Kyle couldn't say anything as tears streamed down his own face. A joy he had only felt once before flowed through him, filling him with warmth. They stayed like that for what felt like a long time, though it must have been only a few minutes.

"It feels so good to finally be home," his mom said, pulling away from him.

For a second, Kyle's heart dropped, and his mom's smile was replaced by compassion. "I know it's not our house, Kyle, but we can't go back. Not with the Rose possibly looking for us."

This had to be their new home. He tried to let the thought sink in. Even though it felt strange, he couldn't actually imagine leaving the academy, now that he was in so many classes. In a way, it did feel like home.

Ocean's dad cleared his throat, and he and Mrs. Sanders exchanged a look. Kyle glanced at Ocean, who had the same look on her face that he probably did.

"Kyle, Ocean, there's a few things we have to tell you. First of all…" Paul glanced at Mrs. Sanders, who nodded. "I want you to know that we've thought really hard about this for as long as we've been together. I don't want you to feel like we don't care about you, but we're adults, and—"

Mrs. Sanders elbowed him, grinning. "You two are going to be siblings! We're getting married."

Kyle just stared at her, frozen.

"Ocean," Paul continued, "we both know how much you miss your mom, and you know I miss her too."

Kyle glanced at Ocean, who was staring at the ground, tears falling down her face.

"You knew—" Paul was cut off as Ocean rushed into Mrs. Sander's arms, hugging her as if she would never let go. Kyle stared at them as his mom bent down, hugging Ocean like her own daughter. He didn't know whether to laugh or cry or run away.

"Kyle, how about it?" Paul said, looking straight at him. "I'm not your father, but maybe you could let me be your dad?"

All Kyle could do was nod.

"All right, that's good enough for me." Paul smiled, slowly walking over to Kyle and putting his arm around him. Suddenly, two more pairs of arms wrapped around him as Ocean and his mom joined the group hug. Finally, someone let go, and they fell apart, Ocean crying, his mom grinning, and Paul giving her a knowing smile.

"Ohh, Kyle, I almost forgot!"

Kyle felt his stomach tighten as his mom opened a briefcase she had set in the sand beside them and removed a tablet from it, handing it to him. Turning his body to block the glare on the screen, Kyle turned it on and froze. For a second, he didn't breathe, then a voice that he recognized so well filled his ears.

"Hi, Kyle," his mother said, smoothing her brown frizzy hair with one hand. She was sitting in a desk chair, with the dark oak door of her office on the *Emerald Wind* behind her. "I honestly hope you aren't watching this. If you are, then you already know why." She glanced down, as if reading something, then looked back at him. "I guess it's probably too late to warn you about the Rose. The fact you're watching this at all means that Fiona or your father is protecting you from them, and you're probably on the run. I want you to know, Kyle, that whatever happens is all part of God's plan."

The screen blurred as tears welled up in his eyes, the sting of longing filling him.

"I want you to know that I love you more than anything in this world. But even though I'm not with you anymore, I'm still alive in Heaven. I can't imagine the pain you must have gone through, and I wish I could be there to comfort you."

She wiped her eyes and slowly continued.

"I don't know where you are or what you're doing, but I want you to know that above all, God loves you. Don't ever let your love for Him diminish." A door behind her started to open, but before he could see who opened it, the video ended. His heart skipped a beat. He looked up to see tears streaming down his mom's cheeks again.

"She knew all along, Kyle, and I—I didn't know."

Kyle stared at her, then looked down at the tablet again. The hand of the person entering the room was visible, and on the wrist was a golden watch with a green bird on the face.

"There's something else, though."

Kyle's head jerked up at Mrs. Smith's voice as she gently took the tablet from him. Without saying anything, she handed it back, and Kyle found himself staring down at a page of names, diagrams, and what looked like detailed plans of some sort.

"Kyle..." She paused dramatically. "This is what we found in your mother's necklace. It's everything she's been working on at the academy."

He almost dropped the tablet.

"Your mother had been deciphering Rose documents for years. When she... disappeared, we thought they were gone—until now. However, these documents only include assignments and names. We still don't have enough proof to shut the Rose down."

"So why are you telling me all this?" he asked, looking up from the screen.

"Because," she replied, smiling at him and Ocean, "these documents tell us where to *find* that proof. Kyle, Ocean, I think it's time you knew about Operation Opal."

IN THE BOWELS OF the *Dolphin Diamond,* a lone shadowy figure stood in the corner, a faint glow illuminating his face.

"I assume the mission was a success?" His thick British accent echoed through the silent room.

"Everything went according to plan. As promised, you will receive your payment," the monotone robotic voice replied. Instead of a person's head like one would expect to be on the other end of a video call, all he could see was a single golden rose floating in a rippling bowl of water sitting atop a marble countertop.

"And what of the boy and girl?" He swallowed, not really wanting to hear the answer. He knew he shouldn't care about what happened to them. That wasn't his job, but still...

"Oh, they're both a bit wet, but alive thanks to agent Conner."

Faraway let out a breath, deciding to ask an even riskier question. "I know it's none of my business, but what exactly was so special about that necklace?"

"I would tell you, but I'm afraid if I did that, I would have to kill you, and neither of us want *that*." The voice gave an evil-sounding robotic laugh as a match appeared in the corner of the screen and a gloved hand touched it to the rose. The flower instantly caught and started burning, the petals curling as they turned black and disappeared. "What I can say is that with your help, we are one step closer to bringing peace and order to a country that has long abandoned such principles. Oh, and Faraway?"

The agent tensed, though he fought to keep his voice steady. "Yes?"

"Try to look a little less like I'm waiting behind you to kill you. I'm not the kind of person who kills for no reason. On the other hand, if you breathe a word of this to anyone..."

Faraway nodded absently, fighting the urge to turn around.

"Good! Then if there's nothing else, I hope our paths do not cross again." The last of the flame petered out, leaving the once gold rose only ashes floating in the bowl.

As the screen went dark, the agent leaned back against a pipe. *Peace and order?* "What have you gotten yourself into this time, James?"

The Aquamarine Files

To whom it may concern,

The book has come to the end. It is over, done. There is no more—nothing past this page—so you may now close the book with that satisfaction of an entirely and utterly complete story. Still here, are you? I suppose that begs the question, "Why?" Perhaps you've fallen asleep because the story was so boring, perhaps you don't believe me, or perhaps you've already turned the page and seen that there is, in fact, more content. If it is the latter, perhaps you did not see the "top secret" stamped on this document. No harm done. You can now close the book—throw it into the nearest ocean and pretend you never saw it. Then again, you could take a peak and I would never know. Or would I...

Name: Kyle Joseph
Sanders
Age: 12
Description: hazel
eyes, dark-brown hai[r]
brown-tinted skin.
Abilities: leadership
Fact file: Kyle lost h[is]
family in a storm on t[he]
ocean, and was adopte[d]
by Mrs. Sanders.
Guardian (Female):
Fiona Sanders
(Adoptive)
Guardian (Male): NA

Name: Fiona Sanders
Occupation:
Free-lance Writing
Description: blue
eyes, dark, blonde
hair, light skin,
tall.
Abilities: writing,
baking, teaching,
cryptology
Fact File: Fiona used
to teach cryptology
at the academy,
however, afer her
friend's death, she
disappeared.

Name: Quin Rose Swift
Age: 16
Description: blue eyes, chestnut hair, darkish skin, tall.
Abilities: athletics, coordination, observation.
Fact file: When she was three months old, Quin posed as a baby during an undercover mission.
Guardian (Female): Terrisa Smith
Guardian (Male): Jonathan Smith

Name: Ocean Sierra Lee
Age: 12
Description: blue eyes, long dirty blond hair, light skin.
Abilities: swimming, creativity
Fact file: Ocean was born with only one leg.
Guardian (Female): NA
Guardian (Male): Paul Lee

If you have read this far, then you already know too much. They will stop at nothing to get what they want. I can't say any more. I already may have told you too much. Below, you will find the keys to codes hidden throughout the book. They will tell you more. Should this code fall into the wrong hands, all would be lost. Guard it with your life.

315°, 90°
45°, 180°
0°, 225°
270°, 135°
90°, 315°
180°, 45°
135°, 0°
225°, 270°
45°, 90°
0°, 180°
270°, 315°
135°, 225°
180°, 90°
315°, 0°
225°, 45°
270°, 135°
0°, 315°
45°, 225°
135°, 180°
90°, 270°
225°, 0°
315°, 45°
180°, 135°
270°, 90°
0°, 225°
45°, 315°

An Interview with Timothy Wolfe

How exactly did you come to write this book?

Contrary to what Timothy Wolfe may have told you, I am not a secret agent, and I did not do extensive research to figure out Kyle's story. It all started a long time ago, in… Colorado. That's right. I started writing a book about the ocean when I lived 1,000 miles away from the nearest one and had never even *seen* that vast expanse of water. Perhaps that's what made it so intriguing, so captivating.

Well, in this desert, surrounded by thousands of miles of land, eight-year-old me decided to write a book one Saturday afternoon (I will note it was not rainy.) I got as far as the first paragraph before I forgot about it, but that spark had been lit. When I was ten or twelve, I took up that story again, and I just wrote.

What is the first piece you ever wrote?

The first story I ever wrote was a picture book about me eating everything. That book has been placed under the highest level clearance, and is never to be shown to anyone. The first story I can share I wrote when I was eight, *Lost at Sea,* which has morphed into the book you are holding now. It looked something like this:

"Ella, Ella, Time to wake up!"cried Tommy.

ten-year old Ella threw off her dolphin covers, sprang to her feet and looked at her turquoise dolphin clock. It was 7:30. the school-bus would be hear at 8:00. she quickly got dressed. Ella and her twin brother, Tommy, raced down stairs. There were fresh steaming rolls on the table. Ella and Tommy sat down and ate.

And it would have continued like that until the end, where Ella turns into a dolphin. Yes, this is an unaltered snippet from my first version. Yes, my character's name was Ella, and yes, I will regret ever letting this snippet see the light of day.

Is it possible for our young readers, some only eight themselves, to write a novel?

Yes, of course! The fact that they're reading this is proof that you can indeed write a novel as a kid and publish it. Yes, it will take lots of time, hard work, and many a tearful night, but if you are truly a writer, then all those things won't stop you, because you love to write and that will drive you to do the impossible, and finish, and maybe even publish, a book.

Who are your favorite characters?

My favorite characters are Quin and Ocean. I love how Quin is always getting herself into trouble with her "leap before looking, then deal with the ground when it gets there," mentality. She's quirky, and extremely stubborn, but she also loves to help others, even above herself. I like Ocean because, even though she's faced so many challenges, she's always upbeat and confidant. Also, like me, she's terrified of water, but also drawn to it.

Who is your favorite author?

My favorite author? I don't have one. I know, it's a cheap answer, but really, there are so many good ones, and they're all good in different ways. I like Brandon Sanderson and James Ponti because they're funny, Wendy Mass because she paints beautiful characters and scenes with her words, S.D. Smith because his fantasy world seems more real than ours sometimes, Peter Jay Black because he's amazing at action scenes, and so on. I honestly can't choose.

What was your favorite part about writing it?

My favorite part about writing is exploring the world "off camera." I like to live in the setting, see what the character sees, talk with the characters, explore an untouched world, and then bring it to our world through words. However, seeing my characters heal and grow is a close second best.

And with that, I'm afraid I have to go. After all, I have a novel to plan, a character to kill, and a butler to frame for it. *tips fedora* until next time.

The AQUMARINE Team

WHILE THERE ARE MANY people who helped to make this book a reality, I want to acknowledge three individuals who really made the book shine. Evelyn, Lucy, and Katja, without you this book would not be what it is today, and so you all have a special space in my book.

Evelyn M. Sweno

Editor, alpha reader, beta reader, critique partner, and fellow young author

Ev has been one of the most influential people in my story (other than my sister). She's been with me since the moment she agreed to read my first draft until the moment I hit "publish". It was rough going, like a ship at sea, but she never gave up, even through storms and waves, and I'm so thankful for that.

Fact file: Evelyn M. Sweno is a student of natural medicine and the writing craft, living— normally barefoot— in rural Colorado. Since writing her first journal entries at age seven, she's been recording stories and gleaning knowledge of the craft from peers' work, like Mission Aquamarine. In her short time as an adult she's attempted to doctor her siblings, smuggled ammunition, and drafted a fictional novel on particularly short people gardening in the plains. Hungry to learn, Ev is on a mission to serve her writer-peers, even if that means crashing Mr. Wolfe's computer a few times.

Katja H. Labonté

Editor and fellow author

Of course, without my wonderful editor, this book would still be tucked in a corner somewhere, afraid to see the light of day. Any good book needs a great editor, and Katja is nothing if not the best.

Fact file: Katja H. Labonté is a Christian, an extreme bibliophile who devours over 365 books in a year, a certified editor, and an exuberant writer with a talent for starting short stories that explode into book series. She's a bilingual French-Canadian and has about a dozen topics she's excessively passionate about (hint: that's why she writes). When she's not editing or writing, she spends her days enjoying little things, growing in faith, learning life, and loving people. You can follow her life journey, find free books, browse her services, and more on her website (katjalabonte.wordpress.com) or her blog (littleblossomsforjesus.wordpress.com).

Lucy Peterson

Illustrator and fellow young author

Without my amazing illustrator, this book wouldn't be what it is today. A story is more than words on a page, it is a doorway into another world, and Lucy has helped me capture that world with more than just words. Her illustrations have truly brought this story to life.

Fact file: As an author and an artist, Lucy Peterson strives to bring stories to life in a way that reflects the beauty and glory of the One True King. When not working on her latest commission, you can find her reading, wrangling her insane characters, or absent-mindedly forgetting the eyes in her latest piece of fan art.

You can connect with her at: thepixiespaintbrush.com

Acknowledgements

I would also like to thank everyone who made this book happen who didn't make it to the Aquamarine Team, but were still invaluable.

First, I want to thank all the wonderful teachers who showed me that writing could be fun. To Mrs. Templeton, Mrs. Zubris, and Mrs. Bard, thank you for doing the hard work to raise up writers that will change the world.

I want to thank my sister and writing partner, Elisabeth. Elisabeth and I have been through many an adventure together, from breaking into private property to discovering a Civil War era cellar, and always taking the path less traveled (for that is where the adventure always is). We've been friends for longer than we can remember, and have always had a knack for getting ourselves into things. Beside that, she's always there to brainstorm and patch holes in my story, and is still wrong when it comes to commas.

I also want to thank my mom who never stopped supporting me on my writing journey and in life. I'm lucky to have you.

To my Alpha and Beta readers, agents Bee, Ace, Sparrow, Snickerdoodle, Sunflower, Avocado, and Kitten. Although you didn't end up in the Aquamarine Team section, your constant help and critique were invaluable. You will always be the true Aquamarine Team in my heart.

To my amazing street team, Wren E. Noellie, Ocie Barton, Serenity F. Helzerman, Emily Brown, Hannah Cahoom, and Emma Runyan, who went above and beyond to spread my story and grow the flame.

And last but certainly not least, I want to thank God, who gave me and my story life, and was always my friend, even when I had no one else. Had it not been for Him, this book would not exist.

CRYTSAL Agency

AGENT PROFILE

PERSONAL FILES:

Real Name:	███████
Code Name:	Agent Wolf
Alias:	Timothy Wolfe
B.O.B:	███████
Nationality:	United States of America
Gender:	Male
Language:	English

FACT FILE:

He has traveled to two different countries, has stopped a runaway motorhome, found numerous secret passageways and an abandoned cellar from the colonial days, broken into private property on more than one occasion, and always takes the path less traveled by, for that is where adventure waits. He's also been in an explosion.

ASSIGNMENTS:

Mission:	Aquamarine
Assignment:	Investigator

LOCATION:

Country	United States
Region:	███████
District:	███████
City:	███████
Street:	███████

Satellite image of last known location
(approximate)

DESCRIPTION:

Age:	20
Hair Color:	Dark Blonde
Eye Color:	███████
Skin Color:	Red-ish tan
Vision:	20/20
Blood Type:	███████
Height:	███████

SPECIALIST FIELDS:

- Graphic Design
- Writing Affairs
- Cryptology
- Terrorist Affairs
- Research

After years of hiding from a clandestine spy organization, Timothy Wolfe has emerged to publish his first novel, Mission Aquamarine. Although no one knows his exact location, reports say that he lives somewhere in the woods on the East Coast, where he allegedly explores secret passages, breaks into restricted areas, and can be found in the remotest of places, often taking the path least traveled. Should you attempt to track him down, you may just find him chronicling an adventure at Crystal Academy, eating a bowl of ice cream with his cat, or reading in some secluded corner. Dydfgbcnpu nh pob ih nb ixxdifh. Kojjoa bcd ejrdh. Sdaifd bcd Bcofp.

www.ingramcontent.com/pod-product-compliance
Lightning Source LLC
Chambersburg PA
CBHW071240300726

48975CB00002B/501